Gordon S. Dickson was born near Inverness, Scotland, but left at an early age when his family returned to Northern Ireland.

He was educated at secondary and grammar schools, but scraped through English "O" level, as essay writing was not his strength.

He was employed in the Civil Service for several years but is now retired and has only recently taken up writing books.

He enjoys reading several genres of books but mainly historical and detective novels, and a little gardening.

Other books by this author are:

Verdict Unknown
Verdict Unknown, the Sequel
The Sheriff of River Bend
Des Pond, Special Agent (Comedy)
The Wartime Adventures of Harry Harris
(a Bartonshire Tale 1)
An Impossible Quest (a Bartonshire Tale 2)
The Life and Times of Victoria-Ann Penny
The Heir...Apparently. A Bartonshire Tale 3.

In memory of Alfred (Alfie) Donnell

Gordon S. Dickson

THE SPANISH ARMADA

WHAT IF IT HAD ALL GONE WRONG?

AUSTIN MACAULEY PUBLISHERS™

LONDON • CAMBRIDGE • NEW YORK • SHARJAH

Copyright © Gordon S. Dickson 2023

The right of Gordon S. Dickson to be identified as author of this work has been asserted by the author in accordance with sections 77 and 78 of the Copyright, Designs and Patents Act 1988.

All rights reserved. No part of this publication may be reproduced, stored in a retrieval system, or transmitted in any form or by any means, electronic, mechanical, photocopying, recording, or otherwise, without the prior permission of the publishers.

Any person who commits any unauthorised act in relation to this publication may be liable to criminal prosecution and civil claims for damages.

This is a work of fiction. Names, characters, businesses, places, events, locales, and incidents are either the products of the author's imagination or used in a fictitious manner. Any resemblance to actual persons, living or dead, or actual events is purely coincidental.

A CIP catalogue record for this title is available from the British Library.

ISBN 9781035806188 (Paperback)
ISBN 9781035806195 (ePub e-book)

www.austinmacauley.com

First Published 2023
Austin Macauley Publishers Ltd®
1 Canada Square
Canary Wharf
London
E14 5AA

With thanks to my cousin Esme Briggs for reviewing the original draft.

Table of Contents

Chapter 1: War with Spain Looms   14

Chapter 2: The Spy Network   21

Chapter 3: The Journey Home   28

Chapter 4: Tragedy Strikes   33

Chapter 5: London Prepares for War   40

Chapter 6: The Situation Worsens   52

Chapter 7: The Queen Consults Sir John Proudfoot   57

Chapter 8: The Invader Reaches the River Thames   64

Chapter 9: The Queen and Her Entourage
           Are Evacuated   70

Chapter 10: The Royal Progress   77

Chapter 11: Warwick Castle Gained at Last   83

Chapter 12: The War Is at a Stalemate 89

Chapter 13: A Turning Point in the War 98

Chapter 14: Have You Ever Been to Ireland? 104

Chapter 15: The Stronghold of Red Ruairi MacLean 112

Chapter 16: The Return to London 118

Chapter 17: The Jury Decides 141

Chapter 18: The Final Moments 150

History records that the Spanish Armada was dispersed and mostly destroyed by winds and storms, but what if history told a different story?

Historical characters, fictionalised, who appear in this story:

Queen Elizabeth Tudor, Queen of England.
King James VI, King of Scotland
Charles, Baron Howard of Effingham, and Earl of Nottingham, the English High Admiral.
Sir Francis Drake, popular English seaman.
King Philip (Filipe II), King of Spain.
Duke Alonso of Medina Sidonia, Spanish commander.
Pope Sixtus V.
Sir Walter Raleigh, English explorer.
Master William Shakespeare, popular playwright.

All the other characters in this tale are fictional:
Sir Thomas Tovey, head of English national security.
Mistress Eliza Helena Askew, spy for Sir Thomas.
Mistress Mary Valerie Brown, also a spy.
Edward, Sir Thomas' secretary.

Miguel, a Spanish soldier in the Netherlands.

General Suarez, Spanish officer in the Netherlands.

Lieutenant Garcia, also of the Spanish army.

Sergeant Edward Jenner, of the London City Guard.

Lady Agnes Appleton, lady-in-waiting to the Queen.

Lady Maud Fellowes, ditto

Lady Frances Meadows, ditto

Sir John Proudfoot, English army officer.

Commander Sanders of the Queen's Guard Regiment.

Charles, Lord Durham, Commander of the York garrison.

Lord Angus Kelsey, Earl of Renfrew, a Scottish lord.

The Chief Herald of Scotland, Sir Angus McTavish.

The Lord of the Treasury, Sir Jasper Penrose.

Sir Percival De Gravlines, the Lord Chamberlain.

Captain Sheridan of the Kent Volunteers.

Pedro Martinez, Captain in the Duke of Medina Sidonia's forces.

Master Dick Hawkins, a stable owner.

Mistress Hawkins, his wife.

Master Bell, their neighbour.

Henry, an oarsman/guard.

Barnaby Adamson, a coach driver.

Sir Robin Hargreaves of Chelmsford, captain of the garrison.

Squire Milner, host to the royal party.

Lady Milner, his wife.

Commanding officer of Warwick garrison, Sir Percy Frobisher.

Lady Margaret, Countess of Warwick.

Henderson, a servant

Captain Sidney Lancing of the Warwick garrison.

Norbert Donaldson, a servant in Warwick Castle.

Daisy Lyttle, a servant in Warwick Castle.

General Hatling, commander of Scandinavian forces.

James (Jamie), son of Harold. A spy for Sir Thomas.

Stanley, Lord Dudley, and 5 friends:

Sir John Archer,

Peter Cranley,

Andrew Gainsford,

Sir William Bedford,

Roger Davenport.

George Alfredsson, a sea captain.

Ruairi MacLean, Irish landowner and also friend of Dudley.

Sir Henry Brocklehurst, the Governor of Dublin Castle.

Captain Fitzallen, of the Dublin garrison.

Captain Black, ditto

Oliver Templeton and Ralph Baker, English soldiers.

Justice Goodheart Williams.

Sir Archibald St. John, prosecutor.

Percy, Viscount de Grange, defence lawyer.

Five of the Jury members:

Sir Leonard Grey, foreman of the jury.

Zechariah Milton,

William Wells,

John Ridley,

Jasper Frampton.

Chapter 1
War with Spain Looms

It was a gloomy time in Tudor England. In the year of our Lord 1588, the land was awash with rumours of an imminent invasion by Spain. Spies had reported troops assembling in the Spanish Netherlands just across the English Channel, and a massive invasion fleet being assembled at ports in Spain and Portugal. Sir Francis Drake had led several ships and attacked this fleet in 1587 causing damage in order to delay matters.

Recent history in England had seen much turmoil and bloodshed since King Henry VIII's break with the Church of Rome: the changes to Protestantism under King Edward VI (1547–53), back to Catholicism with his older half-sister Queen Mary I (1553–58), and a return to Protestantism once again under their mutual half-sister Elizabeth I in 1558. Much blood had been shed during these years. Repeated plots and rebellions kept everyone on edge. The state security service was kept busy.

Queen Elizabeth, the last of the Tudor monarchs, was now some thirty years into her reign, most of it spent under threat from Spain and of Catholic uprisings and plots at home. She had spies and informants in every town. Several plots had been uncovered and the plotters executed.

***

In a small square in a poor part of London, a drunken mob was attacking anyone believed to be Spanish, which amounted to any person with a dark complexion. Agitators egged them on, and the victims were pelted with filth and mire from the gutters. It mattered not to the mob that their targets were often as English as they were. Alcohol-fuelled hatred and prejudice precluded rational thought. Something or someone threatened the country and so someone must pay!

The sergeant, Edward Jenner, in charge of a small military detachment of London's City Guard was trying to restore order. The rioters outnumbered his men, so he ordered some to prepare their muskets and the rest to draw their swords. Muskets were duly loaded, propped on a supporting stand for the weapons were heavy, and the swords drawn. The soldiers were apprehensive, for none wanted to open fire on their own citizens, as they blew on the "match", a smouldering cord, to keep it burning. This would be used to ignite the gunpowder charge.

A young woman, who had been mistaken for being Spanish, had been dragged from her horse and was being assaulted. She fought back with the nearest object she could find, a carving knife from a butcher's market stall. The meat had been scattered when the stall had been overturned, and dogs, and a few humans, were seizing their opportunity for a meal. The humans availed themselves of the rare chance to taste meat and slunk away with their booty.

Swinging the knife in a panic, the woman cut the arm of one aggressor and slashed the throat of another. Blood from the man, a burly, unkempt person, spurted out as he desperately tried to stem the flow. Rapidly his life ebbed away and he fell to the ground. The crowd of attackers backed off and stood as if transfixed, then they grew even angrier.

'She's murdered him, she's murdered Edmund!' a female voice screeched.

'Get her, string her up. Hang the Spaniard,' cried another, and the crowd began to step forward. The young woman knew she was in a perilous position and waved the knife desperately.

'Stay back,' she cried. 'I'm not Spanish. I'm as English as you. Stay back.'

The sergeant, seeing her danger, ordered his men to fire a volley over the heads of the mob and to surround the woman. 'Take her into the barracks for her own safety,' he shouted. The crowd, seeing the swords, lost some of their bravery and parted to let them through.

'We'll get her later. You cannot protect the murderess for ever,' the butcher, in a dirty, bloodstained apron, shouted.

The soldiers slammed and bolted the barracks' gate behind them and as they entered the building.

'Lock her in a cell for safety. It was self-defence but that mob will never see it that way,' ordered the sergeant, as the shouts of the crowd faded. They had turned their attention to other badness, namely the looting of unguarded shops. Why waste a good riot? Market-stall traders had hastily packed up and left.

The young woman, Eliza Helena Askew by name, sat down on the rough bed in the cell. She was shaking with fear. Then she stood and grasped the bars of the cell door.

'Help me. They'll murder me. I have an important message for Sir Thomas Tovey.'

'They'll not be getting near you in here, don't worry,' the sergeant said kindly as he locked the cell door. 'It is only to keep you safe. You are not under arrest.' The woman nodded her thanks.

***

Early the next morning, the soldiers were breaking their fast with what food they had, some stale bread and cheese and small beer. New supplies had not materialised as the mob had ransacked the supply waggon, so nobody was happy. They were seated around a rough wooden table, grumbling.

'Bring some to the young woman,' the sergeant said, and a corporal stood and was about to do so when there was a loud banging at the gate.

'Open in the Queen's name,' a voice demanded. A soldier went across the small yard to the gate and peered through a viewing hole.

''Tis Sir Thomas himself with a half dozen cavalrymen,' the man shouted to the others who were in the doorway.

'Let him in, let him in. Quickly now,' ordered the sergeant.

They all stood to attention as the door was opened. Sir Thomas Tovey, head of Queen Elizabeth's security service, entered brusquely with several men. Another man held their horses outside.

'Call out if the mob returns,' Sir Thomas ordered.

'Yes, Sir,' the soldier replied. *Why am I always the one left holding the horses?* he thought.

'I am informed that you have a young woman, Mistress Askew, in custody, Sergeant,' Sir Thomas said loudly.

'Aye, Sir Thomas, that we have. We saved her from a mob last night. Risked out lives, we did. Thought it was best to lock her in a cell, for her own safety,' the sergeant replied. *How did he know who she is and where she was?* he wondered.

'Well, release her, at once,' ordered Sir Thomas. A soldier lifted some large keys on a ring and went to the cells when the sergeant nodded.

'She be dead, Sir!' the man shouted moments later, and he ran back to the main room.

'Dead? She cannot be dead,' the sergeant gasped.

'She be stone cold, Sir. Dead as a codfish,' the soldier replied, and they all rushed down to the cell. Sir Thomas went in to where the body lay and felt for a pulse.

'She's dead all right. How could you let this happen?' he demanded.

'She was alive and well when we left her, Sir. About midnight it was,' replied the sergeant.

'Look here,' a man said, 'there is a dagger in her back.' He had turned the body on its side as he had noticed a red stain on the bed. 'Must have been thrown through the window and she fell back on the bed.' A small window without glass and with an iron bar in the middle was high on the wall.

The sergeant stepped forward and pulled the weapon from the body. 'Hmm, an unusual weapon. Expensive. Whoever owned this was not some ragamuffin in a mob, Sir Thomas. A man of some wealth, I'll wager; or an assassin paid by a wealthy person. 'Tis looking like it is foreign made, Sir Thomas. Well-crafted indeed. A Spanish blade of quality if I am not mistaken,' the sergeant said. 'A fine blade from Toledo and no mistake.'

'Hmm, looks like the hand of a spy sent by King Philip, or a homegrown traitor,' said Sir Thomas. 'I shall take it until I can investigate further.' He wiped the blood off on a blanket and put the dagger in his belt.

'Why would the Spanish wish the death of some ordinary townswoman?' the sergeant wondered aloud. The other man had returned to his breakfast.

Sir Thomas said, 'You might as well know, but keep it between us, that she was spying on the Spanish army encamped across the Channel. She, and another woman, had only returned yesterday, and were due to report to me. I wondered why they never appeared. Now I know.'

'There was no other with her when she was attacked. And now we shall never hear the report,' the sergeant shook his head slowly as they moved back to the front room.

Just then a messenger arrived having ridden frantically to find Sir Thomas. 'Sir Thomas, I have dire news,' the man said as he dismounted and ran to the door.

'Well, out with it, man,' Sir Thomas replied.

'A body has been recovered from the Thames. We think it is of Mistress Brown who was with…'

'Who was with our agent in the Spanish Netherlands, the woman in the cell,' Sir Thomas finished the sentence. 'The assassin has been thorough. Search the body in the cell to see if she has any papers on her person,' Sir Thomas ordered. This was quickly done.

'I found this paper, Sir,' said a soldier a few minutes later. He handed over a small roll of paper.

'Hmm, it is in a cypher,' Sir Thomas said. 'I'll return to my headquarters and have it decoded immediately.' He started to leave. 'Remember, all of you, not a word to anyone of this. Dispose of the body without fuss. Should the mob return inform them she has been taken to the Tower for interrogation.' And he left with this entourage.

'How am I to dispose…?' the sergeant began, but Sir Thomas had mounted his horse and ridden away.

Chapter 2
The Spy Network

Two months earlier in the Spanish Netherlands:

Mistress Eliza Helena Askew, then known by the assumed Spanish name, *Señora* Isabel De Santos, who had been smuggled into the Spanish Netherlands aboard ship, had arrived in a small town nearest the camps where Spain was amassing an army. She was accompanied by Mistress Mary Valerie Brown, known as Maria, posing as her lady's maid, who was pretending to be dumb as she spoke only a little Spanish and could not manage the accent. Sir Thomas had supplied an ample quantity of captured Spanish gold and silver to sustain the two women. "Isabel" was playing the part of a wealthy Spanish lady.

This gathering army consisted of Spanish troops but also many mercenaries. Gold bought the loyalty of many.

Eliza Askew, born at the time Queen Elizabeth ascended the throne, was a tall woman aged thirty, hair black as a raven's wing and with a light brown skin. Her deceased mother had been Spanish and her father was a wealthy English squire, so she spoke both languages fluently.

Sir Thomas Tovey had entrusted her and her companion with this vital mission.

'It is vital we have as accurate an estimate as possible of their army, but be careful,' he said.

For the next two months, Eliza and Mary had visited the army encampments searching for Isabel's "missing husband", *Don* Pedro Miguel De Santos. Both ladies took a mental note of the numbers of soldiers as near as could be estimated.

'No, *Señora*, we have no man of that name on our payroll. Are you sure he is in the army? The navy perhaps?' an officer at the first camp suggested.

'No, he has a dread of the sea, Captain. He is in the army somewhere. He has abandoned me and our children,' Eliza replied, and she dabbed an imaginary tear with a kerchief. Such was the usual conversation in each camp. The two women went away looking downhearted but inwardly rejoicing. They made a note of what they saw.

Back at the inn where they were staying, they encoded their latest information. 'We have but one more camp to visit and then back to England, Maria,' said Eliza happily. She used "Maria" to avoid any inadvertent mistakes which would betray them both. Eliza and Maria always spoke softly in case they were overheard.

Next morning, they set off in a hired pony and trap to the final army camp. It was the biggest yet and tents and shelters covered acres of ground. 'This looks interesting,' Maria said as they approached the gate.

'*Alto*, who goes there?' demanded the Spanish sentry presenting a halberd. (An axe and spike mounted on a long pole.)

'I am *Señora* Isabel De Santos and I wish to speak to your commanding officer,' Eliza said in her most imperious voice. 'Kindly direct me to his tent, young man.'

'I regret I am not permitted to let anyone enter, *Señora*. Tight security and regulations. I'm sure you will understand,' the sentry replied. *More than my life's worth,* he thought.

'Well, I am not under your regulations. Where is his tent?' Eliza demanded firmly.

'If you care to wait here, I shall send a message to him, the General.'

'Oh, very well, if you must!' Eliza replied, impatiently. She snapped open a fan and fanned her face vigorously in pretended annoyance. Maria sat quietly pretending to be bored and uninterested.

The sentry called another man over and sent him to the general's tent. 'Miguel, go to the general's tent and tell him a *Señora* wishes to speak with him.'

Presently, Miguel, an ordinary soldier, returned and said, 'The General Suarez will see you, *Señora.* Please follow me,' and he helped her down from the trap. Eliza gathered her dress to avoid the much-trampled muddy ground and walked with as much dignity as possible. Recent rain had not helped the muddy surface.

'General, Sir, here is the *Señora* who wishes to speak with you,' said the soldier as he entered the tent. A tent much larger and better furnished with every luxury than the others.

'Wait outside,' said the general to the soldier. 'Please come in and take a seat, *Señora.*' Eliza did so. 'How may I help you?' asked the General smiling, or rather, leering at her.

He stroked his well-groomed goatee beard. He had his own personal barber with him on campaign.

Eliza felt revolted by his sleezy appearance, but replied graciously, 'I am seeking your help in tracing my husband, Don Pedro Miguel De Santos, who has abandoned me and our children. Left us destitute. I am certain he may be one of your officers.' She produced a kerchief and wiped imaginary tears.

'Do not upset yourself, dear lady, I shall help if I can. What is his name again?'

Eliza repeated all the information about her "errant" husband.

'I am not familiar with that name. My adjutant, Lieutenant Garcia, will search the pay records for him. You must understand there are many thousands of troops here,' said the general and he ordered the man to do just that. He left the tent and went to the paymaster who was in an abandoned cottage. 'A glass of wine, while you are waiting, *Señora* De Santos?' asked the general.

'Indeed, that would be most welcome, Sir. After the rain this morning, it's become a rather hot day, don't you think?' She fanned her face.

'Yes, it is. It is to be expected in July though, even here far from our beloved Spain,' and the general poured two glasses of finest red wine from his personal supply. Suarez did not see why being at war should deny him a few luxuries.

'As I have said, my husband abandoned us, myself and our four children, and I need to trace him. I had to leave them in the care of my aunt and uncle. I have, shall we say, limited resources and finances are low,' said Eliza, looking suitably forlorn.

'I'm sure we will find him if he is here. Another glass of wine, *Señora* De Santos?'

She took a sip. 'Hmm, no, perhaps not. It is a pleasant vintage, General, but I have to drive the pony and trap back to town. My maid, Maria, is not good with horses, and is too timid to try the reins. She drove us into a ditch once!'

'I understand.'

The tent flap opened. 'Ah, here is my adjutant returned,' the general said. 'Well, what have you found?'

The adjutant entered the tent and said, 'I'm afraid not much, Sir, *Señora*. We have a Pedro De Santos, but he is only seventeen years of age. With respect, *Señora,* he is too young to be your husband.'

'Yes, he would be,' Eliza smiled. 'Well, gentlemen, I'm sorry for wasting your time. I shall leave you to your important work, fighting the hated English I presume. May God bless your endeavours,' and she raised her glass and drank another sip of her wine.

'Yes, I'm sure we will prevail, *Señora*. We have more than enough troops to prevail. Lieutenant, see the *señora* to her carriage.'

'Yes, Sir, with pleasure,' said the adjutant and he smiled broadly. 'He was considered handsome and fancied himself as a ladies' man. Eliza forced herself to smile.

'Thank you for your time, General, goodbye.' She offered her hand, and the man kissed it, and she exited the tent and made her way to the pony and trap. The adjutant helped her up to her seat and said farewell. Eliza started the pony moving and it trotted off down the road. The soldier clicked his fingers, and a corporal joined him.

'Have a man change into civilian clothing quickly and follow them. I have the feeling they are not as they seem. The enemy are sure to have spies around. We cannot be too careful.'

'Yes, Sir,' the man replied and saluted.

***

Once they were on the road and out of earshot, Eliza asked Mary what she had seen.

'As near as I can estimate there are twenty thousand men encamped judging by the number of tents. Assuming each holds about six men. I could only glimpse the cannon but there must be hundreds of pieces. Many sizes, but mostly quite large,' Mary replied. 'And I got the impression they will be moving in a matter of days. A man said something which I think means five days, *cinco dias*?'

'Hmm, yes, well done. We shall write this up in a cypher and return to England forthwith. A ship is to be awaiting us each evening from dusk until dawn just off the coast at Knokke-Heist. With luck, we will be home by morning,' Eliza said. Mary was pleased at the thought of home.

'I shall be glad to be home again,' Mary said. She reached into a small bag where they had some flasks of water. 'Would you care for a dri…?' Her voice trailed off. 'Eliza, there is a man on a horse behind us, about half a mile off. Do you think we are being followed?'

'Surely, you are mistaken. I hope so anyway,' Eliza replied. 'Don't let him see you have noticed him.'

'Don't worry, I won't. We must be careful though. He could have overtaken us easily but is riding rather slowly.'

'I shall stop by yonder brook and you can water the pony and see what he does. If he goes ahead past us, he is just a traveller. If not, then he is suspect. How does that sound?'

'Good idea. I am the maid, after all, so he would be suspicious if you were to do the work,' Mary said and smiled.

Eliza brought the pony to a halt at the stream which ran beside the road for a short distance. Mary alighted taking a wooden pail with her. While filling it, she glanced back towards the horseman. Then, lifting the pail up to the pony's mouth, she said, 'He has stopped and moved behind a tree out of sight. So, there is no doubt, we are being followed.'

'Hmm, I was afraid of that. That general was too friendly. He made my flesh creep.' Eliza shuddered at the memory. 'He must have suspected something and is hoping we would lead his man to other accomplices.'

'There is nothing we can do but continue. We shall return to the village inn as quickly as possible, then get two horses and head for the rendezvous point on the coast tonight. That soldier must eat sometime, so if we see him move from observing the inn we shall leave,' Eliza continued.

'Sounds like a good plan,' said Mary and she threw the pail back into the trap and climbed aboard. Using a small mirror she noticed their follower also came back onto the road. Eliza tried not to seem hurried but could not wait to get back to the inn.

Chapter 3
The Journey Home

Once they had returned to the village inn the two women obtained food and wine, and secretly packed some for the journey to the coast to rendezvous with a ship, which would take most of the night hours. They feared they might even have to wait for the following dusk if the ship had left.

Mary, glancing through the window, noticed the soldier hiding behind a cart across the street. She kept well concealed while she waited patiently for him to move for food, or a call of nature.

Around ten o'clock that evening, which was a moonless night, all went quiet. Eliza, who had taken over the observation point, noticed the man slip away and enter a nearby inn which was still open. The two women immediately headed for the stables where two mounts had been prepared. A few silver pieces had ensured the ostler's co-operation, but he was a loyal Fleming anyway and hated the Spanish invaders.

At midnight, the two fugitives checked for a sign of their watcher and then left by a small gate at the back of the inn. They rode astride as side-saddles were unavailable. The ostler gave them directions for getting out of town unseen, and after giving him a few more coins they trotted northwards towards the coast. They were on a little used road, barely more than a track, to avoid meeting Spanish troops, or those who might inform on them.

Meanwhile, the soldier on watch had discovered they had fled. He had questioned a patron coming out of the inn who had noticed them leaving in a hurry. He galloped back to the camp. A troop of six horsemen at once set off in pursuit.

On one occasion, the women heard the sound of the hoofbeats of horses in a hurry on the dried earth road, as the sound travelled far in the night stillness. They guided the horses into some thick undergrowth, dismounted and stroked the horses' noses to keep them quiet. Minutes later the six cavalry men galloped past.

'That was too close,' Eliza said after holding her breath.

'We'll have to take another route as soon as possible,' Mary suggested.

When, after another league, they came to a crossroads, they turned north-east as they saw the men some distance ahead heading west towards the French border.

A large crucifix stood at the roadside. The cross leaned at an angle because an overloaded hay wain had brushed against it, and an arm of the Christ-figure was hanging loose. ''Tis a bit askew, like me,' Eliza murmured and smiled. Mary chuckled.

An owl hooted in the darkness. 'No one asked your opinion, Master Owl,' Eliza said. Mary stifled a laugh.

Several hours of riding brought them within sight of the coast. Eliza stopped her horse at the top of a hill, or what resembled a hill in the flat coastal area. 'I cannot see any vessels out there,' she said to Mary as she peered into the early dawn mist.

'Nor I, Eliza. Perchance we are too late, and they have already departed ere daylight comes. Or there could be enemy vessels in the vicinity.'

'The arrangement was that they would stay while it was still dark. I'll strike a flint to this tinder and see if there is a response.' She struck a metal blade on the flint and after a few tries the tinder began to smoulder. 'Hand me some of that dry grass, Mary, please.' The dry grass flared into a flame and soon a small fire was burning on the ground. Mary threw some twigs on it. They waited for three minutes but there was no response from out at sea.

'It's no good,' said Mary, 'we've missed them.' They both felt troubled.

'We shall have to…No, wait! Do you see yonder light?' Eliza gasped. ''Tis about a half league distant.' She hid and exposed the flame several times with a coat as a signal.

'Yes! Yes, I see it. Let's make haste and get to the beach,' Mary exclaimed. She covered the flame with sand to conceal their presence.

Once on the beach they spotted a ship's boat rapidly approaching. 'Ahoy, is that "Deliverance"?' asked a male voice using the password.

'Yes, "the package is ready",' Eliza replied. The rowboat grounded and a sailor helped them aboard. The horses' saddles and harness were removed, and the mounts were set free. If they were found, they would be taken as strays hopefully. The tack was dropped into the sea.

'We are most pleased and thankful to see you, Captain,' Eliza said as they climbed aboard the ship, the Albatross.

'And I you, Mistress,' the captain replied. 'We had almost given up hope of seeing you these many nights. Now, we must away quickly.' He turned to the first mate and gave a series of orders. Soon the sails billowed, and the vessel began to move, gaining speed rapidly. The breeze was favourable.

The Spanish riders, which the women had seen, appeared suddenly on the beach. A few fired their muskets at the ship out of anger as it was too far out to sea to have any effect.

'You are too late, *Señors*,' Mary shouted, mockingly.

***

'Yonder be our destination, Ladies,' the captain said some hours later. 'London, fairest city as ever was, in my opinion. And my opinion is the only one which counts,' he chuckled.

Some lights could be seen in the distance where early risers went about their business. The two women had slept for most of the voyage, and it was now full daylight. The captain said, 'I shall release a pigeon to inform Sir Thomas.' A sailor released a homing pigeon, it circled for a while then headed for London.

'At this moment, I can only agree, Captain. I am longing for dry land. I am not a sailor,' said Mary, looking decidedly green from seasickness.

'We must hasten to our destination; the safety of England is at stake,' Eliza said as they prepared to disembark. The ship was moored, and the gangplank lowered into place. 'Many thanks to you and your crew.' They took their leave and waved from the dock as they mounted two waiting horses. Sir Thomas Tovey had prepared things well.

No one noticed two figures, in dark cloaks and hoods, astride two horses in an alley.

Chapter 4
Tragedy Strikes

The two women made their way towards the pre-arranged rendezvous in a tavern near St. Paul's Cathedral, "Ye Crosse Inn". It was near St. Paul's Cross, a well-known open-air preaching pulpit.

Sir Thomas Tovey was already there, waiting impatiently. The message by homing pigeon which had been sent from Canvey Island to Tovey's headquarters, when the ship had been sailing up the Thames estuary, had arrived at the loft, and the message taken to Sir Thomas. He preferred to contact his spies in random venues to avoid enemy agents.

Unfortunately, the two women never arrived. The two hired assassins following them chose a deserted alley between some warehouses to make their attack. They rode their horses straight into the women's own steeds which shied and reared up. Mary was thrown backwards and fell heavily to the cobbled street. Her skull cracked audibly, and she lay still. Eliza, a better horsewoman, was able to regain control of her mount and, unable to aid her companion, rode off as quickly as she could. It was vital her message reached Sir Thomas, or all was lost. *I should have sent the cypher by the pigeon,* she thought. She glanced anxiously behind her.

One of the attackers pursued her while the other searched Mary's clothing for any concealed papers. He then threw the unfortunate woman's corpse into a tributary of the Thames and followed his accomplice.

Eliza's horse came to a halt when she was stopped by a mob, as recounted previously, which was seeking any supposed Spanish persons. She was surrounded and pulled by rough hands from the horse which bolted off down the street. Eliza's pursuer reined in and watched what would ensue. As we have seen, she grabbed a knife and sought to defend herself. 'Unhand me, you knaves,' she cried, 'stand away. I am about the Queen's business!' The mob just laughed.

'A likely story. Grab the Spanish witch. Don't let her escape,' shouted an uncouth lout in shabby clothing. He and water were strangers.

'Stand back!' Eliza shouted again as she slashed two men with the knife. Just then the City Guard arrived, and she was rescued.

By the time, Sir Thomas arrived next morning Eliza had been murdered by the assassin who had followed her. He was in the employ of the Spanish ambassador who had his own network of spies.

***

At his headquarters, Sir Thomas waited impatiently while Eliza's message was deciphered. 'Ah, at last,' he cried, as he turned from staring out of the window when his secretary entered the room. He took the transcript and read it eagerly sitting down at his desk. 'It is worse than we had feared, Edward. The invasion is imminent and, if these figures are correct, a Spanish army will overwhelm our defences. I must away to the palace at once.' He grabbed a cloak and hat and shouted out of a window to a stableboy to prepare a horse. A bay mare was saddled for him.

He arrived a short time later at Whitehall Palace where the Queen was staying. She rarely stayed long in one place but frequented several palaces: the Tower of London, St. James' Palace, Greenwich Palace, Hampton Court, Richmond and Nonsuch palaces, as well as Windsor Castle. This was to confuse any would-be assassins sent by Spain, or homegrown traitors.

'Ah, Sir Thomas, do you bring me good news?' Queen Elizabeth asked gaily. Her face was covered in white makeup with lips, cheeks and eyebrows enhanced. A red wig covered her sparse natural hair. It did not make her attractive, but no one dared to say so.

Sir Thomas knelt and kissed her outstretched hand. 'I fear not, Your Majesty. Your realm is in gravest danger. Greater than anyone feared.'

'How so, Thomas?' she enquired. Her gaiety evaporated.

'A huge army, Majesty, is assembled across the Channel. According to my spies, who have been murdered, the host against us is fearful indeed. Much larger than we had estimated.'

'Murdered? How then did you obtain this information?' the Queen looked puzzled.

'In brief, Majesty, one lady, Mistress Askew, had to be rescued from a mob by the City Guard. She was in a cell for her safety, as was thought, but a dagger was hurled from a window, and the unfortunate woman perished. A cypher was found on her body though, and it revealed the Spanish plans. Here is a copy prepared for yourself, Majesty.' He handed a paper to her. 'We have an estimate of the numbers. But there will also be many troops on their ships coming from Spain. Over one hundred ships, I am informed. Galleons, veritable wooden castles, it is said. Our small vessels have tried twice to stop them, but storms in Biscay have plagued our efforts.'

The Queen stood and strode irritably up and down while she read the note, her elaborate dress in the "drum" French farthingale fashion, swishing back and forth. 'Even the weather favours the wretched Spanish King. Hmm, summon our counsellors and the Captain of the Queen's Guard, and our naval commander at once. We must defend our coast. Where are they likely to land, do you think?'

'It could be almost anywhere on the south coast, Majesty, or even up the Thames,' Sir Thomas replied. 'However, I am sure barges full of soldiers would take the shortest route. Have we a map to hand?'

The Queen shouted for a map to be brought. There was a lot of hustle and bustle as servants sought a map.

A servant hurriedly laid a map of the south-east of England on a table. The Queen's ladies-in-waiting weighted the edges down with sundry objects.

'See here, and here, Majesty.' Sir Thomas indicated probable spots. 'There are wide beaches and no cliffs. Were they to get landed and organised they could march on London within hours and arrive in a matter of days. I have taken the liberty, Majesty, of sending orders to your castles on the coast to prepare to resist. Cannon are to be sited at likely landing places as the castle commanders think best.'

'Very good. Well done, Sir Thomas. The invader must be stopped at all costs,' the Queen slapped a hand on the table. 'Ah, here are my officers. Gentlemen, what are your arrangements to stop this invasion?' she demanded, and Sir Thomas repeated his assessment of the danger.

A leading officer offered an opinion. 'Majesty, we can muster an army at each possible site, but it will spread our resources thinly. Would it not be better to have all our men in one place and to march them quickly to where the enemy fleet is heading?'

Sir Thomas replied, 'That would risk the enemy getting a foothold. They might even land at several sites. Our men must be closer and drive them off. Artillery and muskets are what are needed.'

'And cavalry. Have we much in the way of cavalry?' demanded the Queen.

'A sizeable number are already moving to Kent, Majesty, but alas not as many as may be needed,' said a cavalry officer of the dragoons. 'You need to require every noble to place horsemen, at their own expense of course, at your command, Majesty.'

'Yes, granted,' said the Queen. She was pleased not to be paying. 'It is time my noble lords did something for our protection. Send my demand at once,' she spoke to a secretary standing nearby.

'Yes, Majesty,' he replied and bowed.

'I suggest the army be stationed at various points around the coast. Swift messengers or signal fires can summon them to a danger spot,' Sir Thomas said.

'Yes, yes, do that,' the Queen agreed. 'What of my navy, Lord Howard?'

Charles, Lord Howard of Effingham, a man in his fifties and Admiral of the Fleet, stepped forward. 'Your Majesty, as you know our fleet is insignificant compared to that of the enemy. Two attempts have been made to stop it, but unsuccessfully. We are at present in the Channel, at Plymouth, and intend to harass it as it continues eastward. Their progress is slow as they have cumbersome ships. Their seamanship is below par, in my opinion.'

'Very well. May God guide your efforts. Do not let me down, my lord,' the Queen said with a lightly veiled threat.

'I shall depart for Plymouth at once, Majesty, with your permission,' Lord Howard replied. The Queen waved a hand nonchalantly to dismiss him.

A coach drawn by four horses immediately left for Plymouth carrying the admiral.

'Which reminds me, get my bishops and clergy on their knees praying for victory, Sir Thomas. It is time they earned their salt,' the Queen added.

'Yes, Majesty.' He smiled. 'It is indeed time.'

'Now, the day is advancing; evening draws nigh. One must away to the Globe Theatre. Master Shakespeare is putting on his newest play. A history of one of my ancestors, I hear.' She chuckled. 'Let us depart, ladies. Sir Thomas, gentlemen, keep me informed of the situation,' and she exited the room brusquely, follow by her attendants.

'Yes, Majesty,' he replied. Sir Thomas muttered quietly, 'Her realm in mortal peril and Her Majesty sallies forth...to the theatre!' He looked up at a portrait of her father, King Henry VIII. 'I wonder what he would do,' Thomas mused.

'Go for a jousting tournament, I shouldn't wonder,' replied a courtier. The two of them laughed.

Chapter 5
London Prepares for War

Next morning.

'Have all the City Guard on full alert, day and night. Store food for a siege in the Tower Fortress for there is a danger the Spanish could overwhelm our army,' ordered Sir Thomas. 'All male citizens to arm themselves as best they can and be prepared to hazard their lives.'

'Yes, Sir,' said an officer of the City Guard.

Sir Thomas addressed Sanders the Commander of the Queen's Guard, 'Move every available man to strategic posts from London around the coast as far as Folkstone. Cavalry units every five leagues and signal beacons on hilltops. Oh, and swift horses prepared to bring news here,' Sir Thomas continued. 'And send homing pigeons to our castles; Her Majesty must be kept informed.' *I hope they don't eat them,* he thought.

'Yes, Sir Thomas,' Commander Sanders replied. 'Our army will be spread very thinly, if I might say, Sir Thomas.' His face was pale and his eyes bloodshot from lack of sleep.

No one had slept properly for days. Rumours spread like wildfire among the populace. Those who could get transport left the city for the north followed by the curses of those left behind.

'Have all the regiments from the north and west reported yet?' asked Sir Thomas.

'Yes, Sir, most have arrived or are underway, all except the border ones with Scotland. It is feared the Scots may seek an advantage if our men are removed. As many as it is safe to do so are on their way. The border garrisons in Carlisle and Berwick are being supplemented with locals from the northern towns,' Sanders replied.

'Very well,' said Sir Thomas. 'Now, we wait for news of the invasion. What news of the weather in the Channel?'

'The latest report from Dover Castle received this morning is that it favours the Spanish should they move soon, Sir Thomas,' said Edward, his secretary. 'A southerly breeze prevails. Even the winds are against us.'

'Oh, for a storm. A veritable tempest,' Sir Thomas cried, raising his eyes heavenward.

'Yes, indeed, Sir. We can only hope,' Edward added, and he took his leave.

Within hours, soldiers from all corners of the Kingdom were tramping the roads of Kent in South-East England. Signal beacons were prepared atop every hill towards London, and cavalry units awaited their summons to an enemy landing. Where tents were not available the men were billeted in churches and large houses. Some owners protested, until informed to resist would be counted as treason. Better a little inconvenience than to lose one's head.

***

Meanwhile, in the English Channel the small English fleet sallied forth from Plymouth to harass the Armada. This was making its way slowly eastwards in a crescent formation. Progress was slow because the larger vessels moved ponderously, especially so because many of the crews were forced into service with no experience, and they were overloaded with supplies and men.

On July 31st, Sir Francis Drake and Lord Howard led the English ships as they made swift attacks on any enemy vessels which broke formation. They relied on heavy cannon fire to do damage, but only two Spanish ships were damaged, due to accidents.

Eventually, the Armada reached Calais on France's north coast and made rendezvous with the army waiting nearby. During that night, the English sent fireships to disrupt the enemy vessels, which cut their anchors and headed to the open sea. None were destroyed by the fireships.

The Spanish regrouped next day and made their way back to Calais and began towing barges full of soldiers towards England. The galleons functioned as a barrier to the English ships and protected the barges. The English ships approaching bow first, firing only two bow-chasers, were outgunned by the Spanish firing broadsides. The English were only able to fire a broadside as they turned back and were largely ineffectual.

Lord Howard urged his ships to make every effort to delay or destroy the enemy fleet, but he could make little headway and he eventually sent a swift vessel to sail for London to carry a warning.

There was, consequently, a great uproar and panic in the capital. Queen Elizabeth made a now famous speech at

Tilbury, in early August, to bolster her troops, 'I have the body of a weak, feeble woman; but I have the heart and stomach of a king, and a King of England too,' she cried. Great cheers followed and her army set off with determination. In reality, the Royal Court and people in authority feared the worst, rule by Philip II of Spain and the imposition of Roman Catholicism, once more, in England. Many remembered vividly the reign of Henry VIII's daughter Mary I, known forever as "Bloody Mary", for the harshness of her rule.

The Spanish army, meanwhile, had begun to disembark along the Channel coast. Those English troops in the area tried heroically to drive them back but to no avail. Cannon placed to overlook the landings tried in vain to deter the enemy. Cannon balls hitting the sand did little harm. The invader quickly unloaded their own weapons which were larger than the English ones, so the defenders were driven back.

Urgent messages were sent to London and to other army units, in order to speed up those still in transit from the north and west. More troops were moved from the Scottish border in the following days. Movement was slow and so the Spanish were able to gain a good foothold on the coast. The English army could do little but be an annoyance.

The Queen ordered the city and the Tower of London to be protected with every cannon available, and for combustibles to be piled at London Bridge, the only crossing, to destroy it if necessary. 'The enemy will have to go many leagues upriver to cross,' Queen Elizabeth declared.

'Yes, Majesty, as you wish,' said Sir Thomas. 'Shall I have the Crown Jewels removed from of the Tower? They must not be allowed to fall into enemy hands.'

'Yes, do so. Where could we send them? I know, have them taken to Warwick Castle or even Kenilworth, and be prepared to move them further if this war goes against us. The enemy must not gain possession of them at all costs. Throw them in the sea as a last resort but keep them from Philip's grasp. Since his marriage to my late sister, he thinks he is King of England. I shall dissuade him of that! The jewels are your responsibility, Sir Thomas. Do not let me down.'

'Yes, Your Majesty,' Sir Thomas replied. He bowed and left, his mind in a turmoil. *My head would quickly leave from my shoulders, should I fail,* he thought. The Queen had similar thoughts about his head, or lack of it.

***

The Scots, seeing the English predicament, mobilised an army to take advantage of the situation. King James VI was descended from King Henry VII of England through a daughter, Margaret Tudor, who had been married to the Scottish James IV. Therefore he, James VI, was already the first in line, the heir, to the English throne, should Elizabeth die childless. This looked very likely as she was ageing and unmarried. James could not resist the challenge.

So, as Spain landed in Kent, the Scots crossed the border at Berwick and headed for the city of York. They met little resistance. The English army could only try to delay the advance. The English commander in York, Charles, Lord

Durham, could do little but hold out as long as possible, for he knew no help would be forthcoming from London.

As they encamped, the Scottish lords approached the king, hoping he was in a good mood.

Lord Kelsey of Renfrew in a Scottish accent said, 'Yer Majesty, we ha'e been discussing this war on England and we are much troubled.'

'And just what is troubling ye, Renfrew? Are we no' in a position to tear Elizabeth from her throne? The greatest opportunity tae do so that we ha'e ever had. We were beaten and destroyed at Flodden Field in mah grandfayther's time. Is it no' time fer oor revenge?' James replied. He quaffed a goodly wine and sampled some roast venison. He threw the bone to his dog.

Angus Lord Kelsey, Earl of Renfrew, cleared his throat. 'Majesty, as ye ken ye will, in all likelihood, be King o' England when Elizabeth dies, hopefully soon...'

'So? She cannae live forever. She is nearly sixty for sure, and wi'oot any bairns.' James grinned.

'So, Majesty, if Philip o' Spain wins this war, he will crown himself King o' England and return that land to Catholicism. His heir will rule after him, so you, Majesty, will be robbed o' yer rightful heritage. Philip wouldnae countenance a protestant succession.'

'Hmm, Ah see yer point,' said King James, stroking his beard thoughtfully. 'Why has nae one thought o' this afore now?' The lords were silent. James continued, 'So, ye, no doubt, would recommend us tae side wi' Elizabeth. Am Ah right?'

'Erm, aye, Yer Majesty. That way there is every chance Spain will be driven intae tha sea, and yer new kingdom be assured,' replied Lord Kelsey. 'As ye say, she cannae live forever.'

'Aye that makes sense. Make it so. Call mah scribe then send mah heralds tae London at once and let us ha'e a peace treaty, on the condition Ah'm recognised as heir wi'oot any prevarication. Speak with Thomas Tovey and get it in writing. Tha English are no' to be trusted,' James declared, and he stood.

'Now, let us dine, my lords, for Ah am much fatigued this evening and would retire early.'

His troops were more "fatigued" as most had walked from Scotland on a forced march.

***

Sir Thomas made the decision that it was more important to drive the Spanish off, and deal with the threat from Scotland later.

The Queen agreed with this. 'The lesser of the two evils, wouldn't you say?'

Sir Thomas grinned. 'Yes, Majesty, you are correct as ever.'

Spain was at the height of its power as Philip was not only King of Spain but also of Portugal and other dominions, including the Netherlands and vast lands in the Americas. Moreover, gold from the "New World" supplied the financial backing he needed. The Scottish army by comparison was a mere nuisance in Sir Thomas's opinion. Many in power disagreed but the Queen backed his judgement. There was in reality little choice.

Some days later as the Queen held an audience the Lord Chamberlain, Sir Percival De Gravlines, approached.

'I beg leave, Your Majesty, to approach,' he said and bowed deeply.

'Yes, you may do so. You look flustered, my lord,' the Queen jested. The courtiers all around dutifully laughed.

'Majesty, the heralds of King James of Scotland are without, and beg admittance for an audience,' said the Lord Chamberlain.

'Heralds you say! From that Scottish King? I had his treacherous mother, Mary, former Queen of Scots, executed some time ago; about a year as I recall. Her own lords had forced her from the throne.

'I recall she was betrothed, aged five, to my late dear brother Edward. We are most fortunate that little liaison never took place. We would all be Catholics, my lords, for she was an ardent follower of that religion.' She laughed sarcastically. The courtiers nodded agreement and laughed too. 'Bid them enter. We may as well hear what they have to say.' The Queen waved a nonchalant hand. *If one can comprehend their tongue?* she thought. *I have had an occasion to hear a Scot speak once and I almost asked for an interpreter.*

The heralds, three in number, in tabards which reached from neck to below the knees, displaying the Scottish Lion Rampant Coat of Arms in red and yellow, entered, bowed deeply and approached the throne when bidden. The chief herald, Sir Angus McTavish, went down on one knee and presented a scroll sealed by King James. The man spoke in heavily accented English, 'Yer Majesty, we bring most cordial greetings frae yer royal cousin, King James, the sixth o' that name, who wishes Yer Majesty a long life.'

'Yes, yes, we are sure he does,' replied the Queen, with a hint of sarcasm. Some courtiers chuckled quietly at this. She whispered out of the side of her mouth, 'I can barely understand his accent, Sir Thomas.' Louder, she said, 'You may tell our cousin, James, we return the sentiment. Does he wish to surrender to us?' Dutiful laughter from her court.

'Nae, Majesty, tha King is aware o' the dire threat tae Yer Majesty's kingdom frae tha Spanish invader, and proposes, therefore, a treaty o' mutual aid. Thus, shall be driven frae this oor mutual island, tha upstart King o' tha Spaniards, and tha mutual threat frae Rome; a danger to both oor Reformed Kirk and the Church o' England. Oor master feels certain Yer Majesty will agree.'

There was an intake of breath from all assembled. Queen Elizabeth turned to Sir Thomas for advice. She whispered, 'What say you, Sir Thomas? Is this some trick perhaps, to catch us off our guard?'

Sir Thomas replied quietly, 'If it be a trick, it is a strange one indeed, Majesty. Your realm can certainly only benefit thereby. Your northern frontier will be safeguarded, and we need all the soldiery we can muster. Methinks the bold James has an eye on this throne in the future. It would be denied him should the Spanish prevail. He is, unfortunately, your heir by succession.'

Elizabeth stood and walked as she pondered what to reply. Standing by a window, she turned to the heralds and said, smiling, 'Well, gentlemen, we thank you for your attendance and we shall peruse what our cousin, James, has written. Sir Thomas shall convey our decision to you.' She indicated for a servant to take the scroll. 'Now, please leave us awhile 'til we prepare our reply. My Lord Chamberlain.'

'Your Majesty?' the Lord Chamberlain said and stepped forward.

'See that these gentlemen are well fed and comfortable while we deliberate. They had better stay here tonight and return north with our answer on the morrow. Have suitable bedchambers prepared.' These rooms had secret passages which allowed the conversations therein to be overheard. The Queen was thinking, *Mayhap we shall learn something to our advantage.*

'Your Majesty, bedchambers have already been prepared. I was sure Your Majesty's generosity would see these gentlemen were comfortable.' The Queen smiled and nodded. The Lord Chamberlain bowed and turned to the heralds. 'If you would follow me, Gentlemen. I am sure you will be glad of refreshments after your journey.'

'Aye, 't would be must welcome, Sir. Thank you, Majesty,' the herald replied.

They all bowed as they left the royal presence. *Och, Ah hope these English Sassenachs are no' goin' tae poison us,* one man thought.

***

'Sir Thomas, what say you to these requests by my dear cousin in the north?' asked the Queen about an hour later. She had pored over each word in the scroll several times.

49

Sir Thomas replied, after perusing the scroll carefully, 'He wants fifty thousand gold pieces to pay his army. And his right to your throne, when Your Majesty departs this world, to be enshrined in law. He must fear he will be blocked from the succession, though the English parliament has never opposed his claim. Nor will they.'

'Hmm, "his right to the throne"! Well, at least he is prepared to await my death, the scoundrel,' the Queen laughed briefly. 'He is my heir, unfortunately. My grandfather made a mistake, methinks, to marry a daughter to a Scot, but that is in God's hands. We cannot interfere with that, so, let him have his "enshrined in law". Let parliament see to it.

'Now, to serious business. His army, such as it is, would certainly aid us greatly.' She stood and started to walk back and forth while she spoke. 'The Spanish invader is advancing on London rapidly. Philip must be stopped, or this sacred realm is doomed.' She sat down again and slapped her hand on the chair's arm. 'Can we raise that amount of gold, which is the question? Moreover, has he any cannon? We need more cannon if we are to resist. Judging by reports ours are no match for the Spanish artillery. It can outdistance any we can put against it.'

Sir Thomas replied, 'Yes, 'tis true, the loss of artillery has been great, Majesty.' He frowned.

The Lord of the Treasury, Sir Jasper Penrose, who had been sitting quietly, spoke, 'Majesty, your treasury is all but empty, the coffers are bare save for dust, what with the fleet and the army in Kent. We could perhaps pay by instalments if King James agrees. We shall need urgent tax increases.'

'Seems we have no other choice, but he must not perceive how low our treasury lies. Draft a reply along the lines of "We must maintain much of our finances to pay our own soldiers at present but can offer him payment over three years", for example. This way we do not reveal the true nature of our drastic lack of funds. You can, I trust, find a diplomatic turn of phrase, can't you, Sir Jasper?' the Queen replied. She looked directly at him as if daring him to disagree.

Sir Jasper cleared his throat and said, 'I shall certainly endeavour so to do, Majesty.' He smiled slyly. 'We can present it to the heralds in the morning. It will take them several days to reach King James in York where, we are informed, he is encamped, and the same to return with his reply, which will buy us some time. At least, a week.'

'Excellent,' the Queen replied, delightedly clapping her hands. 'Away you go, and start writing, Sir Jasper.'

'As you wish, Majesty,' he replied, bowed and left. *I cannot see any harm in this alliance, but time will tell*, he thought.

Sir Thomas was thinking the same. *I shall tell the Scots on the morrow that I favour this alliance greatly.*

Next morning, Sir Thomas decided to accompany the heralds as far north as Luton, where he remembered he had to conduct some business with a local lord.

Chapter 6
The Situation Worsens

'Your Majesty, I bring dire news,' said Sir Thomas a few days later entering the room breathlessly.

'Well out with it, Sir Thomas. Can things be any worse?' Queen Elizabeth replied. She had even given up attending the theatre. Most of the company of actors had left London for safer cities. Acting as a brave soldier was more acceptable than actually being one.

'Your Majesty, our army has been unable to confine the Spaniards to the coast. The castle at Deal has been overrun, and Dover is under siege. Alas, there is little hope of raising the siege. The garrison is reportedly eating rats, so low are supplies. Fortunately, their last pigeon has been sent here.' He raised an eyebrow.

'Your troops are managing to hold the invaders in the South Downs where the hills give our cannon some advantage, but our men cannot hold forever, I fear,' Sir Thomas replied. 'The enemy guns are heavy and difficult to move speedily. Our gunners have been instructed to kill as many of their oxen and horses as possible. Thank Heaven for our muddy roads.'

'We need the Scottish army more than ever, much as it pains me to say it,' the Queen said. 'Has there been any reply from James?'

'It is reported from Watford that his heralds are approaching London. They should be here within a few hours, Majesty,' said Sir Thomas. 'I received a message via a pigeon.'

The Queen replied, 'Thank God for pigeons, wonderful creatures. Let not the Scots see us in a panic, my lords. As far as the Scots are concerned, we are winning this war.'

'Yes, Your Majesty,' Sir Thomas replied. He thought, *If only we were.*

'Hmm, have everything in the path of the Spanish destroyed. Leave nothing that would be to their good,' ordered the Queen. 'What is it called by the military? A scorched earth?'

'Yes, Majesty, I have already ordered all iron foundries in the area blown up. No point in giving the Spanish the wherewithal to make cannon balls,' said Sir Thomas.

'Excellent, excellent,' declared the Queen as she stood and began strutting back and forth. 'Thomas, I want you to go immediately to Kent. Make certain all that can be done is being done. I shall give my signet to you. Use it to enforce your orders should any question them.' She removed a large ring from among many adorning her fingers and handed it to Sir Thomas.

'I shall use it wisely, Your Majesty. I will leave at once and put Sir John Proudfoot in charge of the defence of London. He is a capable young man. London Bridge is already prepared for destruction should the worst happen. This will give Your Majesty time to leave for the north and safety. The occupants of the shops and dwellings on the bridge have been evacuated. Some were reluctant to leave and have had to be removed by force.'

Old London Bridge, the only river crossing at that time, was lined all the way across with dwellings and shops.

'It pains me to contemplate running from King Philip,' the Queen said. 'My father would not have contemplated such an event. But our people need me alive and free, so, I shall do as you suggest, should it become necessary.

'Ah, here is James's herald.' She resumed her throne as the herald approached and bowed.

'Yer Majesty, Ah bring ye good tidings from mah King, James tha Sixth o' that name, King o' Scotland and...'

'We know him of whom you speak, sirrah. There is no need for all this folderol. Just tell us what he is proposing to do,' Queen Elizabeth spoke sharply. She was in a bad mood.

'Ah beg Yer Majesty's pardon,' said the herald. 'Tha King agrees tae yer offer tae pay tha sum requested in stages. He is aware o' the expense a war incurs. His Majesty has put his army at yer disposal and has returned tae Edinburgh. Tha entire army is approaching London at this very moment.'

'Excellent, excellent, thank you, my Lord Herald,' declared the Queen. The herald exited.

'Sir Thomas, issue orders, or shall we say, advice, to the Scots as to where you wish them to deploy.' She chuckled at her little jest, and the courtiers dutifully joined in. The Queen looked around to ensure they did so. 'We are sure they will be a deterrent to the Spanish.'

***

Sir Thomas later addressed the herald, 'Good Sir, Her Majesty is pleased with King James's cooperation in this crisis. Please return to Scotland and convey her thanks, and mine.'

'Ah shall, my lord. With yer permission, Ah shall leave forthwith,' replied the herald. A footman escorted the Scot from the room.

The Queen said, 'Sir Thomas, be on your way. Our kingdom's safety is in your hands. Do not let us down.' She did not smile.

Aware of the veiled threat, he bowed and left. He was wearing his best armour with a plumed helmet under an arm.

Having arranged for the Scottish army to follow when it reached London, he made his way to Ashford, Kent, which was the centre of the defensive line set up to hold the invader. The artillery was just managing to slow the enemy advance, but Sir Thomas could see little hope of resisting for long.

Canterbury, which was only five leagues distant, had recently been overrun by the Spanish, and a Catholic bishop, who had accompanied the army, had celebrated a full *Te Deum* Mass in the cathedral.

Anglican prayer books and Bibles were burned. Queen Elizabeth was enraged when she learned of this. The Church of England cathedral clergy had just managed to escape in time as their lives would have been forfeited.

***

'I fear, Sir Thomas, we will have to withdraw to the Thames ere long,' said an officer of the foot regiments. 'We are trying to defend too wide a front line. The enemy is too easily forcing us to retreat, and is receiving reinforcements daily, by all accounts. Were it not for the hills we would have too easily been surrounded.'

'Yes, I understand,' replied Sir Thomas. 'Hold the line as long as possible. I shall send a messenger for reinforcements. All is not lost.' *Yet,* he thought.

Chapter 7
The Queen Consults
Sir John Proudfoot

The Queen, in Whitehall Palace, was beside herself with anger. 'Summon Sir John Proudfoot,' she ordered.

'He is at present arranging the placing of our artillery at the Tower, Your Majesty,' said the Lord Chamberlain.

'Well, get him here without delay. I am most perturbed; I slept but little this past night.'

'At once, Majesty,' replied the Lord Chamberlain. He ordered a messenger to attend Sir John forthwith.

Sir John was a taller than average man for that time, a man a head taller than his peers, with dark shoulder-length hair, a neat beard and a soldier's physique.

Presently, a breathless Sir John entered the throne room, removed his helmet, and bowed deeply. 'You sent for me, Your Majesty?' he said. 'My apologies for the delay, Majesty.'

'Yes, I did. You are here now; that is all that matters. What are the arrangements for the defence of our city, Sir John?' the Queen demanded to know.

'Cannon have been placed on all sides of the Tower's walls, Majesty, and on the city walls. We have secured some from Windsor. The Tower is the strongest and most easily defended strongpoint. As you know, the bridge is prepared for destruction should the enemy approach that far,' said Sir John. Everyone knew it was only a matter of time before this happened.

'Yes, very good. I think my court should take residence in the Tower. It is our strongest palace as you say. The others, apart from Windsor, have little to offer for defence. Do you agree, Lord Chamberlain?'

'Yes, Majesty,' said the Lord Chamberlain, 'what about moving to Windsor Castle, Majesty? It has strong walls,' he suggested. 'Its walls have never been breached.'

'No, no. It is too far from my people. They will lose heart if one is not in their midst. Besides, as Sir John says some of the cannon have already been removed. See to it at once that all the Court is moved to the Tower,' ordered the Queen.

'Very well, as you wish, Majesty,' the Lord Chamberlain replied. He bowed and left.

'Sir John, you may return to your duties. Have some of the artillery from our other palaces moved to the city and the Tower. Keep us informed of any untoward developments.'

'Yes, Majesty. I shall do that. God willing, we shall prevail,' Sir John said, and he took his leave.

Yes, God willing, we shall prevail, she thought.

***

As we have noted most of the cannon and the military complement at Windsor had been moved to the Tower. Supplies of food were also transported.

Sir Thomas Tovey, meanwhile, had consolidated all the army in Kent between the Surrey Hills and the Thames at Dartford. This formed a last barrier to the Spanish. He made plans for evacuating as many as possible across the bridge should the defence fail.

He asked the chief officers of the army, 'Are all our men in position?'

'Yes, Sir Thomas. All is as prepared as can be,' replied Captain Sheridan of the Kent Volunteers, an amalgamation of what was left of several regiments, plus many civilians who joined to fight. Farmers had been forced to leave their land and livestock. Most animals had been seized to feed the two opposing armies.

Sir Thomas said, 'Very well, we can do no more for the present. The enemy will no doubt renew their attack on the morrow. They have received a bloody nose, but are far from giving up, I fear. Rest the men while they can. Have food served just before daybreak. Now, I must attend Her Majesty and report the situation. Someone prepare my horse.' He looked worried. A servant rushed off to the stables.

'Yes, Sir. Breakfast before dawn,' said the captain and he exited the headquarters, which had been set up in a large house in the village of Croydon.

***

'What was that?' Queen Elizabeth exclaimed as she sat in a window seat chatting with her ladies-in-waiting. They were doing embroidery, but none really had the heart for it.

''Twas lightning, Majesty,' one lady, Lady Agnes Appleton, a widow, replied as they all jumped to their feet and retreated into the room. Thunder followed.

'Oh, I do hate thunder. It is so frightening. It sounds like cannon fire,' said Lady Maud Fellowes. Another flash of lightning appeared as she spoke. Lady Maud's husband was with the army, Captain Henry Fellowes of the Royal Artillery.

Another peal of thunder and they all screamed and ran to the far side of the room. Lady Maud almost fainted.

'It is only a storm. Let's play at cards to pass the time,' the Queen suggested. 'Light more candles. It is getting dark.'

'Yes, let's,' Lady Agnes agreed, and she went to a drawer for a pack.

Then the rain began. It lashed down. Folk in the street ran indoors and the rain washed all the detritus into the drain, which ran down the centre of the street.

'I have never seen such rain in all my days, and I'm past forty,' said a butcher whose shop was in Ludgate Hill. His wife agreed.

'Yes, Husband, it be like the days of Noah and no mistake. We ought to go to prayer. Come children join with us,' and their brood of four girls, Abigail, Catherine, Charlotte and Jane, and two boys, Gerald and Thomas, gathered around and knelt on the stone shop floor.

***

'Your Majesty, some wondrous news,' said Sir Thomas as he entered the Queen's drawing room.

'What might that be, Sir Thomas?' she asked as she gazed out at the deluge.

'The rain, Majesty, the rain. The Spanish army is bogged down. They are unused to such weather, being from a dryer clime. Our spies report their heavy guns are immovable. We have successfully attacked with sword and pike and slaughtered many of their gunners. Muskets are of no use as the gunpowder is too easily dampened. Their artillery men are an easy prey and many of their cannon have been spiked, making them unusable.'

'That is good news indeed. Can we foresee victory at last, Thomas?' she asked.

'Alas not, Majesty. I do not wish to be pessimistic but our reports from the south coast say that their commander, Alonso, the Duke of Medina Sidonia, has had thousands more men and supplies brought in from the continent.'

'What are we to do then? Is all lost, Sir Thomas?' the Queen demanded to know as she paced about wringing her hands.

'No, no, but our commanders have proposed harrying them as long as possible whilst our soldiers and artillery are brought across the Thames. They are then to destroy all bridges for leagues along the river. With the river in spate and flooding its banks, Majesty, it will be impossible to cross for days if not weeks,' said Sir Thomas. 'Freshets from tributaries are making flooding the worst in living memory.'

'That is all very well, but what then? All will be lost when the rain ceases,' said the Queen getting angry. 'Even in England the rain does cease occasionally.'

'By then, the Scots and our reinforcements from Wales and the north will be deployed. Our iron foundries are working night and day producing cannon and muskets, and men are being trained in their use; gunpowder stocks have been brought in from the shires. We can resist the enemy, Majesty.' He refrained from mentioning that a clumsy recruit had thought it clever to dry a barrel of gunpowder near a fire!

'Hmm, that is all very well, but our army is finite. What did you say they call him, the Spaniard?'

'Medina Sidonia, Majesty,' Sir Thomas replied.

'Medina Sidonia has limitless mercenaries from all of Europe to hand, should he need them. I'll warrant the Pope is backing this to the hilt. A chance to stamp out this protestant isle,' the Queen replied.

'Yes, that is so, but I have sent requests to the Scandinavian countries for aid as I mentioned to you a few weeks ago, Majesty. The Swedes, Norwegians and Danes have promised men as soon as possible. It will just take time for their armies to assemble. We can still win,' Sir Thomas declared. 'We need not despair, but things will be difficult for a while.'

'Good, good. What of Ireland? Can we bring some of the garrison from there?' the Queen asked.

'That might be problematic, Majesty. The Irish have wind of the invasion, and our commanders are expecting attacks on our castles in the Pale and in Ulster at any moment. Carrickfergus and Dublin can be supplied by sea, but the inland castles are more vulnerable. The commander of Trim Castle has reported much activity from armed men in the area. If the Spanish are defeated here, then the threat to our garrisons, hopefully, will be no more.'

'Hmm, let us hope you are right, Sir Thomas. Let us hope you are right.' The Queen waved a hand in dismissal, and Sir Thomas withdrew.

Chapter 8
The Invader Reaches the River Thames

The rain eventually abated and the roads, such as they were, began to dry.

The Spanish army had been reinforced by more troops from the Continent. Their commander, the Duke of Medina Sidonia, was pleased to be on the move again; his supply of top-quality Spanish wine was almost used up. His many servants were relieved when several new barrels arrived, for their master was unbearable at such times.

Sir Thomas entered the Queen's audience chamber and bowed. 'Your Majesty, I fear I bring bad news.'

'Well, what is it? Out with it, man,' she almost yelled. She was in a foul mood.

'The enemy is almost at the Thames, Majesty. I have ordered Sir John Proudfoot to destroy the bridge when the rear-guard of our men are across,' Sir Thomas said. As he spoke, a series of explosions could be heard.

'I assume that is his work, Sir Thomas,' the Queen replied, coldly.

'Erm, yes, Majesty. A necessary act, unfortunately. Every crossing has now been destroyed for twenty leagues upriver,' Sir Thomas said. 'A detachment of soldiers has been placed at strategic points where the river narrows.'

The Queen thought for a moment, sipped some wine and spoke, 'We are sure our cousin, James, and our reinforcements from the north and west will be in place before long. See that they are well situated to prevent the enemy crossing. You can be sure the Spanish will not stop now, so we, that is you and my commanders, Sir Thomas, must drive them back. Thus far have they invaded my realm, but no further. Do you hear me, Sir Thomas? Do I make myself perfectly clear?'

'Yes, Majesty. It shall be as you wish. Not a Spanish foot shall cross the river.' He was not as confident as he sounded.

***

The Spanish headquarters at Tunbridge Wells, south-east of London.

'My lord Duke, our army has managed to cross the river at a place named Kingston,' reported a captain, Pedro Martinez, to the Duke of Medina Sidonia. He had just finished his siesta that afternoon.

'Ah, music to my ears, Captain. We shall rename it, let me think, King Philipstown. That has a good sound to it. We could even rename the river.' He chuckled. 'How was this crossing conducted?' asked the duke. 'I thought all the bridges were down.'

'Some of our men swam the river under cover of darkness and collected a number of boats. There are many boatyards which had been abandoned. The stupid enemy had not thought to destroy the boats. All our men had to do was tie them together and row across the river towing them all. Then they arranged them together to form a pontoon bridge. Our carpenters had many planks prepared, and by dawn sufficient troops were across to hold the English until we had thousands of men in place,' the captain replied. 'The cannon, being heavy, are more of a problem. They must await the construction of a proper bridge.'

'Excellent, excellent. Ensure a new bridge is started immediately. I shall ride there presently to see for myself; but first a cup of wine to celebrate, eh, Captain?'

'A goodly wine is always welcome, my lord,' the captain grinned. He was unequalled in his consumption of any wine available.

***

Queen Elizabeth was, predictably, enraged at the news. 'They have crossed the river at Kingston-upon-Thames! How was that allowed? Heads will roll for this. Heads will roll, Sir Thomas, starting with yours if you do not supply a solution.'

'Majesty,' Sir Thomas gulped, 'the foe managed to acquire boats and built a pontoon bridge in the night. They had an advanced party across before they were spotted. Our local garrison was no match for them. I have ordered most of the Scots to the area...'

The Queen interrupted. 'Let's hope it is not too late, then. Take as many men as can be spared from the London garrison and send them upriver. And prepare for our urgent removal north if necessary. I will not be a prisoner in my own realm.' She knew what her likely fate would be.

'There is more, Majesty.' Sir Thomas looked pale.

'More! What else, pray tell?!' replied the Queen. She was furious.

'Erm, the Spanish have looted and burned Hampton Court Palace...'

'What?' The Queen felt faint and called for some water. She sat down before she spoke. 'Burned the Palace? Burned my late father's pride and joy? Someone will pay for this, mark my words. Why am I surrounded by incompetence? See to it, Sir Thomas. Find out who was responsible? I cannot believe this is happening.'

'Yes, of course, Majesty. I shall deal with it at once.' Sir Thomas bowed and hurried away. He was relieved to still have a head to bow!

'Prepare my jewels and dresses for urgent travel,' she ordered her ladies. 'We may have to depart in a hurry if these fools do not stop the invader. See to it. I need wine. Bring me some wine! And send for my physician. I feel rather faint.'

'At once, Majesty,' said a lady-in-waiting, and servants scurried here and there packing trunks. Most of the Queen's dresses were decorated with pearls and jewels.

The distant sound of cannon fire drifted through an open window.

'And close that confounded window!' Elizabeth ordered. 'Oh, my head aches. Where is my physician? Why is he not here? Does no one care that I suffer? Does anyone care?'

A lady replied, 'He has been sent for, Majesty. He will be here presently.' *I hope,* she thought.

***

Meanwhile, the English and Scots armies had stopped the Spanish advance at the village of Hanwell not far from London. Fierce fighting had exhausted both sides and the environs were littered with the dead and dying. A truce was called in order to remove the dead and wounded.

Richmond Palace, south of the River Thames, fell victim to the rampaging enemy and was looted. Elizabeth was further enraged by this news as it was one of her favourite residences. The deer in the hunting park were butchered to feed the troops.

A long convoy of carts and waggons ferried the English and Scots wounded into London to the safety of the walls. Many citizens were so frightened that they packed what they could carry and started walking north. Women and children were allowed to leave but all men able to fight were ordered to remain. The elderly and infirm were trundled in barrows or on stretchers.

Sir Thomas reported to the Queen. 'Your Majesty, your army is holding the enemy for the moment, but as thousands more of the enemy are crossing the river every day we cannot hold them for long. Once they get their cannon across then it will be even worse. If only the troops promised by Norway and Denmark were to arrive. They are our only hope.'

'You mean all is lost without them?' asked the Queen.

'Yes, Majesty. I would recommend that you leave the city and retire to Warwick or even further north. Hopefully, our allies will be here before the invader progresses that far.'

Chapter 9
The Queen and Her Entourage
Are Evacuated

For a week, the English and Scottish forces resisted the Spanish in the countryside west of London. Eventually the commander, Sir John Proudfoot, ordered all the remaining men to retreat behind the city walls. The casualties of dead and wounded were too much. Mass graves were dug in every available spot.

'Your Majesty, I beg to report that our forces are greatly diminished and exhausted,' said Sir John, 'without fresh troops there is no hope. I would recommend that you move to a safer location immediately.'

'Move? You mean I should run like a scared puppy?' the Queen roared. Sir John quaked.

Sir Thomas intervened, 'Majesty, it is the most sensible move. Sir John is correct. You cannot risk being taken prisoner by the Spanish. Your death would surely be the result, and our men would lose heart.'

'Hmm,' the Queen mused. 'Where to, I pray you? Where could I flee to? I will not give the Spanish King the satisfaction of seeing me running away.'

'Majesty, he would have greater satisfaction to witness your execution,' said Sir Thomas.

'True, I suppose. Well, if I must, I must.' The Queen pondered for a few minutes then she asked, 'How could I and my ladies-in-waiting leave London without being observed? The Spanish could have spies around the city.'

'There are two options, Majesty,' said Sir Thomas.

'Which are?' asked the Queen.

Sir Thomas cleared his throat. 'First option, by coach, which is slow and easily intercepted. The enemy could have patrols which have evaded your army. With all your ladies and baggage, I fear for the worst.'

'And the other possibility?' The Queen drummed her fingers on the arm of her chair.

'By boat, Majesty.' The Queen and her ladies were in a panic.

'By boat?! There is at least one Spanish ship, the *La Trinidad*, reportedly blockading the Thames. We would never get past it to the sea and going upriver is out of the question.' The Queen was angered. 'Impossible.'

'You could, in the Royal Barge, rowed by eight men,' Sir Thomas replied. 'The barge would have to be kept as light as possible, Majesty. You could only take two of your ladies and a minimal amount of baggage.' He emphasised minimal. The Royal Barge was a long narrow boat with a canopy at the rear for the Queen and guests and the oarsmen at the front.

'Only two of my ladies? Impossible, I need them all. I will not leave one behind.' The ladies were greatly perturbed. 'And what about the servants?'

'The other lady, and the servants, can leave by road, Majesty, hopefully safely, but, as I said, the barge must be light. Tonight is predicted to be moonless and cloudy. It is ideal. You must leave tonight or not at all when the tide recedes.' Sir Thomas was hoping the Queen would see sense.

'Let me think,' the Queen said, and she began to pace up and down the room. She pounded one fist into her other palm. Finally, she said, 'Yes, I agree. Lady Agnes and Lady Frances shall accompany me. Lady Mary, I regret you must accompany the servants and go by coach.'

'As you will, Majesty.' Lady Mary curtseyed. She was relieved because she detested water having been nearly drowned as a child.

The Queen resumed, 'I must insist, however on bringing my jewels, Sir Thomas.'

'Yes, of course, Majesty. We shall need to purchase a coach and horses once we reach Essex so some silver would be preferable. But now, I must away and see the barge is prepared. Lady Agnes, please see to it that all is ready by nightfall.'

'Yes, Sir Thomas,' Lady Agnes replied and curtseyed. She and the other two set about organising everyone. They were very efficient and soon all was prepared. They had indeed been secretly preparing for such an eventuality.

Sir Thomas had already ordered the barge to be made ready. All unnecessary ornamentation was removed. A black cloth was draped over the canopy and bright paintwork was repainted black. The volunteer rowers were issued with dark clothing and soot to darken their faces. The oars were muffled with sacking.

At nightfall, the Queen and her two ladies made their way to the water-gate, known as "Traitors' Gate" for good reason, by many, as those condemned arrived at the Tower by this entrance.

The "minimal" baggage was loaded aboard. Too much in Sir Thomas's opinion but he let it pass; there was no time to argue the point. 'Now, I must impress on everyone the need for absolute silence.' They all nodded. 'Right, you men, cast off.' He spoke to some watermen standing by.

He then placed a black veil over his face. The Queen and her two ladies did the same. It was thought unbecoming for the nobility to use soot.

Slowly the barge edged out of the dock onto the river and the steersman directed the boat downstream towards the sea. The tide was on the ebb which helped.

Meanwhile, Lady Mary and staff left by a gate in coaches or on horseback. Several carts were loaded with the Queen's "necessary" baggage. This consisted of almost all her finery and wigs which she considered "essential".

All was silent as the barge crept towards the Spanish ship which was acting as a blockade. No vessels had reached London for weeks. Sir Thomas put a finger to his lips to indicate the need for absolute silence. The oarsmen were particularly careful.

A weary sentry on *La Trinidad* yawned and leaned against a cannon. His eyes drooped and he thought if he just closed his eyes for a minute he would be refreshed. All was silent and no officers were on deck as he glanced around. *Too busy eating and drinking I'm sure,* he thought. His eyelids drooped.

His eyes stayed closed for several minutes, longer than he had intended, during which time the barge slipped past in a slight mist and headed for the Essex coast on the north side of the estuary. Those on board held their breath.

The sentry jerked awake and yawned. He looked around fearing an officer might have seen him, but all was still. He felt relieved and peered into the darkness. All was quiet. No one was watching the seaward side of the ship as no vessels had tried to reach the city for weeks, and the lone sentry felt it was not worth bothering to look downriver.

The oarsmen on the barge bent their backs to gather speed.

When they were out of sight of the Spanish ship, a mast and a small sail were jury-rigged as a breeze was beginning to arise, and the barge headed for the small port at what is today called Southend. Once they landed an old, dilapidated coach was bought from a sleepy stable owner roused from his bed. He stood shivering in his nightshirt. He had thought of using the old coach for firewood and was pleased to have some coins for it. The boat's crew were given horses and muskets to function as a bodyguard. A bewildered stable owner was left with a bag of gold and no idea whom he had just encountered. The strangers, in plain dark clothing, remained hidden by veils. The owner was too tired to think clearly so took their money and the offered barge without argument. The party then headed north towards the small Essex town of Chelmsford.

Next morning, the man, Dick Hawkins, wandered out in his nightshirt to have a look at the barge which was tied to the dock beside his stable. He scratched his head and rubbed his eyes. 'Wife, Wife, do make haste and see this,' he cried. 'Am I seeing things?'

'What be the noise about? Can a hard-working woman not get a moment's peace?' She had been up a while and lit a fire to prepare breakfast. Her mouth dropped open. 'What is that?'

'Looks like the Royal Barge it does. You remember we saw it at the May Day fair last year when we was in London a-buying horses.'

'So it is. But it be all black, Husband!'

'Those grand ladies last night must have been the Queen and her attendants, and some lord,' the man replied. 'Who else would be in yonder barge?'

'Lord, have mercy, the Queen, and us half-dressed and never bowed nor nothing.' The wife felt faint.

'Never mind that. That lord said we could sell it,' said the man. His face brightened.

'And just who do you think would buy it, with them Spaniards all over the country?' asked his wife. *I'm married to an idiot,* she thought. *More brains in a dead mule.*

'Hmm, well I shall paint it up like new, and who knows what the future holds.' He grinned. 'And there is all this gold the Queen gave us. I'm for buying a new pair of galligaskins.' (Fashionable britches.)

'And I shall have a new bonnet…nay, two new bonnets, and mayhap a matching cloak, with fur trim,' his wife said, and they both laughed. They did a little jig around the dock, singing like drunken sailors.

Mr. Bell, a neighbour, looking out of a window, thought they had taken leave of their senses.

'Must have had a tad too much ale, I'm thinking,' he said to himself. 'Well for them has cash to spare on ale.'

Chapter 10
The Royal Progress

The royal party had continued northwards towards Chelmsford during the night. Progress was slow due to the poor roads – mostly muddy tracks – and the coachman, Barnaby Adamson, insisted on driving slowly. 'If we lose a wheel, we will be in dire straits for certain,' he commented to any who would listen.

At first light, they had a meal at a small inn, and Sir Thomas then sent a rider ahead to see if all was well in the town, which lay a short distance away. They could smell the smoke from cooking fires.

The man re-joined them in a short time. The roads were now dry, so he was not detained by mud.

'Well, young Henry, what have you to report?' Sir Thomas asked.

Henry dismounted and removed his cap. 'Your Majesty, Sir Thomas, I encountered no sign of the enemy, and the captain in charge at Chelmsford said all was safe as the Spanish have been held just north of London. At least, that was the latest news he had obtained.'

'That is excellent news. We should arrive within the hour,' said Sir Thomas. 'The army are doing well in London it seems. We shall beat the invader yet.'

'Let us make haste,' said the Queen. She was finding the travelling rather tiresome, and sore on her posterior due to the roughly made coach.

When they arrived at the town the captain of the local reserve regiment, Robin Hargreaves, had rooms and food prepared for them all. The Queen was not a frequent bather, but she was pleased with a large tub of hot water before she ate.

'Ah, that is much better,' she said. 'Fetch my red dress; the one the Earl of Essex gave me, as we are in Essex.'

'Your pardon, Majesty, but the trunks with most of your dresses were sent by road to Warwick. 'Tis feared the Spanish may seize them,' said Lady Agnes.

'What? Well, fetch something. Am I to wear only my undergarments? Hurry.' The Queen was in a foul mood.

'Yes, Majesty.' The ladies had had experience of the Queen's temper. She was known to often "box someone's ears".

An hour later the Queen, her ladies and Sir Thomas sat down to dine. The food was not as elaborate as in a palace but was devoured eagerly none the less. Nothing but a few bones remained.

'I shall retire for a nap,' said the Queen. 'At what o'clock shall we depart, Sir Thomas?'

'At two of the clock, Majesty. We have a long way to go ere we gain Warwick Castle.'

'Very well, call me at one,' and she flounced from the room, her ill humour abated.

Everyone curtseyed or bowed to the retreating back of the Queen.

'I shall rest too,' said Sir Thomas. 'I would advise you all do the same.' Her ladies followed the Queen. With full stomachs and feeling tired, they helped the Queen prepare for her nap and were soon sound asleep themselves.

***

At two o'clock, the party was preparing to leave. The Queen stopped and spoke to the captain of the guard, 'May I borrow your sword, Captain?'

'Yes, of course, Majesty,' he replied and unsheathed the weapon, wondering what was to happen. He handed it hilt first to the Queen.

'Kneel, Captain,' she said. The captain went down on one knee. 'For your faithful service and providing for the comfort of your monarch, I dub thee Knight of this realm.' She touched the sword on each of his shoulders in turn. 'Arise, Sir Robin of Chelmsford.' Everyone cheered.

The new knight was speechless. Then he recovered and said, 'Thank you, Your Majesty. I am only glad I could be of assistance.'

'Let us away,' said the Queen, smiling, and she climbed into the coach.

They went on travelling to the north-west towards Bedford, intending then to turn west to Warwick. Sir Thomas sent scouts out to ensure no Spanish cavalry were in the area.

He estimated it would take four or five days travelling to reach Warwick. Longer if the horses needed prolonged rest, for no one knew if replacement horses could be obtained on the route.

Repeated rain showers turned the roads into rivers of mud and the team of horses became exhausted.

'Your Majesty, if we cannot obtain more horses soon, progress will be impossible,' Sir Thomas said.

'It is most annoying, I must say. It is bad enough contending with an invader without our own weather fighting against us too,' the Queen replied. 'Oh, for some sunshine!'

'Hmm, I quite agree, Majesty. The Spanish we at least can oppose, but the weather…!' Sir Thomas replied.

They moved slowly for another league when there was a loud "crack" and the coach lurched to one side. A front wheel had caught in a rut breaking two spokes.

'Are you all right, Majesty?' Lady Frances Meadows asked anxiously.

'Yes, yes, I am perfectly well. Thank you for your concern. 'Tis but a bruise. My dear mother lost her head. Someone help us out of this contraption,' she shouted. The Queen had banged her head on the side of the coach, which was lying at an angle. The other two ladies were unhurt, just shaken.

'Some of you men help Her Majesty out,' Sir Thomas ordered as he was pinned under Lady Agnes who had been thrown on top of him. Three men climbed onto the side of the coach and forced the door open. Soon, all were safely extracted and stood on the roadside. The Queen lost a shoe in the mud leaving her stocking sticky with the mud. A soldier retrieved the article and wiped it as clean as possible.

'Thank you, young man,' she said. 'This is intolerable, Sir Thomas. As soon as this war is over something must be done about our roads. What say you?'

'Most certainly, Majesty,' Sir Thomas replied. 'We should erect toll booths to pay for it, I suggest.'

'Yes, and now send someone to find a smithy to repair this wheel,' said the Queen. 'I recall we passed one a few leagues back. Give the smith this silver for a speedy repair,' and she handed over ten silver pieces.

Two men left with the wheel, a small one about the size of a modern car's, slung between two horses.

The coach was of a basic design common at that time, a rough wooden cabin with a door and two windows on each side, the glass was broken, with four small wheels and no leather springs. Very uncomfortable for passengers and driver. The coachman sat on an outside seat in all weathers.

The men were away several hours, even though the smith hurried to obey the Queen's command. The bag of coins helped! He had never seen so much at one time in all his days. The two men were tempted to keep some of the silver for themselves but feared the Queen, or Sir Thomas, finding out.

Eventually, the party resumed their journey, but night was already falling. A man rode ahead, and spotting a large house among some trees he ordered the occupants to prepare beds and food for the travellers. Squire Milner and his wife were in a panic when they learned who was coming, and quickly ordered the servants to prepare. Several fowl were hastened to their doom.

An hour later a weary and bedraggled group descended from the coach and quickly devoured the proffered foodstuff. Hot water and comfortable beds helped the ladies to refresh themselves and soon all were asleep. Sir Thomas was also accommodated in the house, but the men bedded down in a loft above the stables.

Next morning the royal party departed after thanking their hosts, who were in a sort of disbelieving state. The monarch had actually stayed in their home! Ever after their main bedchamber was referred to as the "Royal Bedchamber" and proudly displayed for every visitor. The squire also was knighted for his services, though it was his wife who did most of the organising.

Chapter 11
Warwick Castle Gained at Last

The next few days' travel passed without major incident. As they approached Warwick, Sir Thomas sent two men ahead to check the lie of the land. They had no idea how the war was proceeding, but country folk on the way had been packing their possessions on to carts in case they needed to flee. Their fear was palpable.

An hour later the two men reported back. 'Sir Thomas, the castle is thankfully still in loyal hands. The enemy is held in a rough line from the Chiltern Hills in the west to St. Albans and Epping Forest in the east. Seems like both armies are fought to a standstill,' one of the men reported. 'Of course, that was the position ten days ago.'

Sir Thomas replied, 'Then let's proceed with all haste, Her Majesty is exhausted. She has had a deal of hardship to endure.'

'On the contrary, Sir Thomas,' the Queen interrupted, 'I have had my eyes opened to the hardships my people have to endure, and to their much kindness. This I shall ne'er forget. Let us hasten on our way. I, their Queen, vow to alleviate their lot.'

The party was soon approaching the castle, which was on a large earth mound overlooking Warwickshire's River Avon. The walls and towers promised safety.

Sir Thomas, looking anything but aristocratic, shouted to a sentry on the wall, 'Open the gate, in the Queen's name!'

'Who dares use the Queen's name, sirrah?' asked the sentry.

'Dare you, man, to impede Her Majesty?'

The sentry, seeing a shabby coach and bedraggled escort, went to his commanding officer, Sir Percy Frobisher, and reported, 'Sir, there is a coach at the gate purporting to be carrying the Queen!'

'Hmm, the Queen indeed! I doubt it but open the gate. I shall call out the guard in case it is a Spanish ruse.' The man ran to the gate shouting for more men to attend. A trumpet sounded.

Moments later the gate opened. 'About time!' shouted Sir Thomas. 'How dare you keep your sovereign waiting! I am Sir Thomas Tovey.'

'Apologies, Sir, but we have to be wary of the enemy – trickery you know,' said the commander of the garrison, who had donned his helmet and best armour just in case it really was the monarch.

'Well, get rooms prepared and food for Her Majesty and her ladies, for me and these stout-hearted fellows. Hurry now!' He indicated the escort.

'Certainly, Sir,' the commander said as he helped the Queen from the coach. 'Majesty, I shall see that your requirements are provided forthwith. Captain Lancing.' He shouted at an officer standing nearby.

'Sir!' replied Captain Sydney Lancing.

'Escort our Queen and her ladies to the castle keep. See that all is supplied at once for their comfort.'

'Yes, Sir,' replied the captain. 'If you would follow me, Your Majesty, ladies?' He had to guess which person was the Queen as all three were equally dishevelled. Fortunately, he addressed the correct lady. Few commoners in those days had a proper idea of how the Queen appeared.

'Lead on, good sir,' the Queen said and smiled. She was pleased to be free of the torture of the coach ride. Her bulky dress had supplied some welcome cushioning.

Captain Lancing said, 'Majesty, I regret my lord, the Earl, is presently with the army, in St. Albans I believe; however Lady Margaret is present. I shall send someone to find her. She usually goes riding of a morn. It being a fine day, at last.'

'No need to bother her, Captain,' replied the Queen. 'Just let her know of our arrival when she returns. At present, all I wish for is a good meal, and a change of clothes. Have some maids attend myself and my ladies if you will?'

'Certainly, Majesty. Please make yourselves comfortable fornenst t'fire. I shall summons some servants at once,' said Lancing who was from northern England and spoke with a regional twang. He threw some more logs on the blaze.

Soon a contingent of maids and cooks was busy attending to the needs of the visitors. Bedchambers were prepared for later and hot water heated by the gallon.

A hearty meal of venison and pork with seasonal vegetables was being enjoyed when Lady Margaret returned from her ride.

'What is the meaning of...?' she began to demand.

''Tis Her Majesty, Sir Thomas Tovey, and two ladies, Countess,' her chief housekeeper interrupted in a whisper. 'They be all travelled from London and demanded food and lodging.'

'Oh dear, I must look a mess. Still cannot be helped so must be endured. The countess put on a broad smile and proceeded towards the visitors.' She made a deep curtsey and said, 'Your Majesty, you do our humble abode a great honour. Have you been provided with all you need?'

'Yes, yes, all is most splendid, Lady Margaret. Please do join us. You must be fatigued after your ride. Fetch another place-setting at once,' the Queen ordered. A place-setting was hurriedly laid for the countess who sat on the Queen's right. 'By the way, have my servants and luggage arrived safely?'

'Yes, Majesty, they arrived some days ago, except Lady Maud Fellowes. I am told she fell ill and has stayed at an inn until she recovers. They had some difficulty avoiding enemy patrols, but all is well.'

'Excellent, and the Crown jewels?' asked the Queen.

'Safely in the dungeon, Majesty. I have the only keys and proposed casting them in the river had the worst happened,' the countess replied. The Queen nodded. The keys were given to Sir Thomas. The countess was truly pleased to be rid of the responsibility.

Soon all were satisfied and sat awhile chatting as the table was cleared. Servants bustled around like bees.

'Now, I do not wish to appear rude,' said the Queen, 'but I would like to rest, Lady Margaret. If you would excuse us.'

'Oh, not at all, Majesty.' The countess looked towards an elderly manservant. The young men had gone to war.

He stepped forward and said, 'My Lady, baths and bedchambers are prepared for all your guests. Their luggage has been brought to the rooms.'

'Excellent, Henderson. Then please have my guests escorted thereto. Majesty, Ladies and Sir Thomas, if you would kindly follow the servants,' Lady Margaret said. 'I bid you all fairest dreams.'

'Most certainly,' the Queen replied, and the party arose and proceeded to their rooms. Blazing fires had been lit and a relay of servants poured gallons of hot water into bathtubs.

Sir Thomas was pleased to be able to relax for the first time since they left the Tower.

Later that evening the royal party re-joined Lady Margaret for supper in the dining room. It was a sumptuous spread. The countess had made sure only the best silver plates and cutlery were on show. A suckling pig had met its end for the occasion.

'Majesty, would you care to try these *po-tay-toes* which Sir Walter Raleigh has lately brought from the Americas? A strange plant as only the roots are edible. Though I do find them quite filling,' the countess said. 'My cook is experimenting with methods to cook them.'

'Oh, yes. I have tried them once or twice before,' replied the Queen. 'Rather an acquired taste I think, but very filling as you say. But, one must say, they are much to be preferred over that tobacco plant he brought. A frightful habit altogether. Burning a smelly, dried leaf indeed. I cannot abide it.'

'I quite agree, Majesty. My husband has been banned from using it,' the countess said with a laugh.

They then adjourned to a drawing room for some convivial chat.

The Queen was indeed in a convivial mood. She rehearsed all the hardships of the escape from London. Lady Margaret and the others listened and listened. Eventually, she could not resist stifling a yawn behind her hand. The Queen actually took the "hint" and said, 'Well, it has been a long day, Countess, and I am certain the servants have need of rest. I shall bid you all *bonsoir*,' and she withdrew. Following a maid with a candelabra she walked to the bedchamber.

Hmm, most unusual for Her Majesty to show concern for servants, Sir Thomas thought, and smiled to himself.

The countess breathed a sigh of relief. Her corset was killing her. She only wore it in company.

Chapter 12
The War Is at a Stalemate

Several battles had been fought just south of Warwick. Battles, some large, some mere skirmishes, had raged at St. Albans, Oxford, Aylesbury and near Hemel Hempstead, which was then a small town. In St. Albans, an ancient Roman town, the fighting was hand to hand in the streets.

The former abbey church, now a parish church since Henry VIII's dissolution of the monasteries, was damaged by cannon balls. (In 1877, it was granted the status of a cathedral as well as a parish church. A unique combination in the Church of England).

A man stood on the tower with two flags. A red one to warn of an enemy advance, and a green flag to signal all clear.

The English and Scots managed to fight the Spanish to a standstill, so both sides sat on their respective hilltops and regained their strength.

***

The number of mercenaries from Europe was rapidly diminishing as people grew disillusioned with fighting in

English fog and rain. Armour and chainmail rusted rapidly in the moist air.

Even encouragement from Pope Sixtus V could not persuade most soldiers. The prospect of fighting in a warmer climate appealed more to many so they went to the Americas. Besides, there was gold in the Americas.

It was now autumn, and the weather worsened. The Britons never thought anything of it, but the Spanish shivered in their tents and dreamed for Seville and Malaga.

The lack of a harvest in southern England meant thousands went short of food. Nor was there seed for the next year. Famine loomed so many country folk trekked north to safer regions.

***

'Great news, Your Majesty,' declared Sir Thomas one cold morning. 'A fleet from Scandinavia has arrived in Grimsby and other ports. Thousands of Norwegians, Danes and Swedes are prepared to help us against the invader.'

'Wonderful news, Sir Thomas. How soon will they be here?' the Queen asked. She had been in a gloomy mood for several days but now perked up.

'A matter of days, Majesty. They set off on the march at once. A mounted messenger has just arrived with the news. It looks like a turning point at last. Praise God!'

'Yes, yes,' said the Queen. 'Get the local clergy on their knees. About time they did something useful, what?' She laughed then added, 'Send this news to our soldiers. It will hearten them, I'm sure. And should the enemy get wind of it so much the better, eh?'

A few days later the Scandinavians, under General Hatling, arrived. They brought with them many cannon and enthusiastic volunteers. Mainly Lutherans they were eager to oppose the Spanish Catholic army.

'Ah, we are most pleased to greet you, General Hatling,' the Queen held out a hand to be kissed.

'It is a pleasure to meet, Your Majesty,' the General replied bowing low. 'We have heard a great deal about you, and your struggle against the Spanish tyranny.

'I have often heard tales of your great beauty, Your Majesty, but the half was not told.' Hatling was what today would be called a ladies' man.

'Hmm, you do flatter me, Sir,' she laughed. Inwardly pleased.

'No, indeed not, Majesty, but I can only apologise it has taken so long to assemble an army,' said the General.

'No matter, Sir. You are here now. Please give Sir Thomas the details of your host and he can distribute them where most needed. Maps have been prepared. We have managed to hold a line for some months, but we could not hold out indefinitely. Now, we can only see the tide turning.'

'I shall do that, Majesty,' said the General. 'With your permission, I shall return to my troops.'

'Yes, certainly, with my blessing. By the way, our revered Admiral, Lord Howard, has reported some small victories over the Spanish fleet. Their great galleons are too difficult to manoeuvre in winter storms and are easier to attack.' (Some had run aground on the Goodwin Sands, a large sandbank mid-Channel, and on rocks.) 'Many have returned to Calais, until spring presumably. So, hopefully that will put a stop to their resupplying their army.'

'Excellent. That is indeed good news, Majesty. Every enemy vessel lost is a gain for us,' the General said, and he bowed and withdrew.

Sir Thomas said, 'With your permission, Majesty, I shall again visit the various camps, boost morale, that sort of thing. I shall, of course, bring greetings and encouragement from yourself, Majesty.' He smiled.

'Yes, Sir Thomas, do that. Perhaps I shall visit some of our men one day soon. I am still a little fatigued after our recent journey.' She sighed.

'Certainly, Majesty. It will be a great boost to morale,' Sir Thomas replied. 'I shall away immediately for this is a great day indeed.' He took horse immediately for the nearest army camp and spent some days there.

***

Gunpowder was running low, so he sent urgent messages to several cities demanding increased supplies. Any manufacturer who failed to do so would be regarded as a traitor, with all that that meant. They all got the message!

Lead from church roofs and grand houses was stripped and melted down for musket balls and cannon balls when iron was in short supply. Spanish cannon balls were dug up and reused. The artillerymen found this a source of amusement: 'They be a-killed wi' their own weapons!' was often said to roars of laughter.

When Sir Thomas returned to Warwick Castle about a week later, he was walking in the garden with the Queen and her three ladies-in-waiting. It was a refreshing autumn day and warm for the time of year, an Indian summer. Lady Maud Fellowes had recovered from her illness.

The party was passing some trees when suddenly an intruder stepped from behind laurel bushes and hurled a knife at the Queen. The ladies screamed and Lady Frances fainted. By chance, the Queen had stumbled over a loose paving stone and swayed forward. Sir Thomas put out a hand to steady her as the knife sliced through her elaborate ruff and embedded itself in a pine tree.

'Alarm! alarm!' he cried. 'Her Majesty is slain!' Several guards rushed towards them with halberds and swords. 'There flees the knave, the assassin. After him, take him alive!' cried Sir Thomas, pointing at the man, as he aided the Queen. A man in rough peasant's clothing was making for a small postern gate, or sally port in the castle curtain wall, to escape. The postern was often used in sieges to allow troops to sally forth and attack the besiegers.

'Seize him!' shouted the officer in charge. 'He must not escape.'

'Take the wretch alive for questioning,' shouted Sir Thomas again. 'I need him alive!'

Two men-at-arms caught up with the would-be assassin and dragged him back to the royal party.

'The Queen is unharmed, thankfully,' said Sir Thomas. 'I feared the worst. Your plot has failed you scoundrel,' he said to the captured man. 'Who sent you? Who paid you? Answer now or suffer. Torture shall soon loosen your tongue, you knave.'

'I shall tell you nothing. I acted on my own to rid England of this imposter queen,' the man said defiantly.

'Did the Spanish send you? Who paid you?' Sir Thomas seized a money bag at the man's waist. He counted out the coins. 'Forty pieces of silver: English coin! Paid by an English traitor then. Our Lord was betrayed for less. Speak, man, and you shall have a quick death. Be silent and you shall die slowly. This I vow.'

The man remained silent. 'Take him a…No wait, let me see that knife.' A soldier had retrieved the weapon from the tree. 'A beautifully crafted dagger. I have seen such before. Majesty' – he turned to the Queen – 'A dagger such as this was used to murder Mistress Askew, one of my spies, just before the invasion. She and another woman had brought me details of the Spanish army.'

He turned to the killer. 'So, I must assume you, you wretch, killed them as well. I repeat, who paid you? Speak!' The man never budged. 'Captain, take him to the castle. A few red-hot irons liberally applied will soon have him talking.'

The captain had two men-at-arms drag the man to the castle. Soon screams could be heard. The blood drained from the faces of the ladies.

'Have no sympathy for him, ladies,' said the Queen. 'There is a traitor abroad who sent this wretch, and he must be eliminated. I foresee a long, agonising death for him, whoever he may be.' She then returned to the castle and sat down to luncheon. The three other ladies ate little.

***

'Stop! Stop! Mercy! I shall tell you all, but only to Sir Thomas,' the assassin cried out after a few minutes. His body, tied to a table, exhibited several livid burns.

'Fetch Sir Thomas,' the captain said to the torturer. The man ran and asked Sir Thomas to come quickly.

'So, as I predicted, you have decided to talk. Who sent you?' demanded Sir Thomas.

The man mouthed words, but no sound was heard. Sir Thomas put his ear near to the man's mouth.

'He says he will tell only me. The rest of you leave. Quickly.' The captain, his men-at-arms and the torturer left the room.

'You, you will keep your promise? You will keep me alive?' the man begged.

'I'm a man of my word, not that you deserve it.'

'And my coins? I want my money returned.'

Sir Thomas grinned. 'As you wish.'

Moments later Sir Thomas called the others back in.

'The wretch has expired. We will not have the pleasure of an execution. He has declared Stanley, Lord Dudley to be his paymaster. It was he who sent him. He is in league with the Spanish. They promised him wealth and position when they gained the throne.'

'Lord Dudley! Can this be true? Are there others involved?' the captain asked.

'I know of no others. The man named no others. He said, "I only ever met with Dudley at his home. But I did get the impression another was listening in to our conversations. It was just a...feeling, nothing more".'

'Now, we must find Dudley, and his possible co-conspirator. Could it be someone at Court?' asked the captain. Sir Thomas shrugged and left the room.

***

'Majesty, the killer has named one as his paymaster,' said Sir Thomas a few minutes later. The Queen and her companions had return to sitting in the garden.

'And who is this traitor who wished me dead? King James? King Philip?' the Queen asked.

'Stanley, Lord Dudley, Majesty, one of your ministers. Paid by Spain, according to the assassin, who has paid with his life.'

The Queen gasped. 'A viper in my closest acquaintances? It is unbelievable. You are certain, Sir Thomas? The man may have lied. Invented this untruth.'

'No, a man who suffered such tortures on his person is unlikely to have lied. Red hot irons have that effect, Majesty. My man did a good job.' Sir Thomas grinned.

'Right, we are unable to bring Dudley to account at the present, but as soon as we win this war he will be tried and executed. Where is he do you think?'

Sir Thomas replied, 'I imagine he will have fled from London. He may well be nearby as he paid that man in silver. I shall organise a search of Warwick and its environs. Who knows what may turn up.

'The man also revealed he got the impression that another was listening to their conversations.'

'Another?' the Queen exclaimed. 'He, too, must be caught. Yes, search everywhere. I want all who were involved. All of them.' The Queen was enraged.

'Now, ladies, let us go indoors for refreshments. Some mulled wine? 'Tis getting rather chilly.' The three ladies agreed wholeheartedly.

Chapter 13
A Turning Point in the War

It was now the depth of winter, a particularly bad winter. Reports from spies said that the Spanish were being laid low by the ague, fever and shivering, as they could not overcome the cold climate. Their army had not been supplied with enough winter clothing as the leaders had expected a quick campaign.

'Sir Thomas,' said one such spy, James, aged sixteen, son of Harold the fletcher, 'the enemy camp near St. Albans is reduced by almost half by my reckoning. They be burning the dead as they are so numerous. I counted nine pyres a-burning this morning. Which is lucky 'cause I can only count to ten, then I run out of fingers,' he laughed.

Sir Thomas laughed too. 'Good news indeed, Jamie. I must inform the Queen immediately. Here, take this purse. You deserve it.' Sir Thomas handed him a purse of silver.

Jamie hefted it in his hand. 'I thank 'ee most sincerely, Sir Thomas. You are most generous.'

'Think nothing of it. Continue your good work and you shall be well rewarded. But take care you do not fall into enemy hands.'

'I will. I go disguised as a country yokel in rags, with a barley straw in my mouth, and leading an old donkey. I pretend to be dumb and just grunt at the Spaniards. They just send me on my way with a kick on my pants if I encounter them,' Jamie replied and grinned. 'Little do they know what be in store for them, if I have my way, Sir.'

'Even so, have a care, my friend.' He patted Jamie on the shoulder. Sir Thomas then mounted his horse and rode to the castle with all haste.

***

'Your Majesty, some excellent news at last,' Sir Thomas reported.

'Hmm, about time. I am longing to get back to London. Warwick Castle is a lovely place but as they say, there is no place like home.' The Queen smiled, and her ladies were equally pleased. 'What is this news?'

'My spy reports large funeral pyres in the enemy camps. The ague is killing them in scores. It seems they had not prepared for the English winter; no winter clothing and they have no resistance to our chills and epidemics. It is surely only a matter of days before they are forced to withdraw.'

'Wonderful! That is wonderful news. Let us drink a toast.' They all raised their glasses. 'To the total defeat of the enemy,' the Queen said.

They all raised their glasses and repeated, 'To the total defeat of the enemy,' and cheered.

And so, as Sir Thomas had predicted during the night a week later the Spanish started on their way to the south coast.

Their ships had been hurriedly docked and the men embarked. Most of the cannon, horses and other equipment was abandoned *en route*. No matter what punishment was threatened by officers the men just left everything. Some could barely put one foot in front of the other.

Some local people lined the cliffs and cheered as they saw the ships depart. Then they proceeded to loot anything of value the invaders had left.

The English, Scots and Scandinavians soon arrived and restored order. All the castles and churches which had been occupied were cleared of any traces of the enemy.

England was at peace, at last.

'Ol' "Jack Frost" has seen off the enemy, brothers,' said one wag. 'A toast: "To Jack Frost"!'

'Aye, to "Jack Frost",' his comrades shouted, as they downed Spanish wine.

***

When the news reached Edinburgh, King James immediately departed for London. He was determined to make sure his claim to the English throne was upheld. A claim which had cost thousands of Scottish lives.

'Ah, Cousin, how pleasant it is to see you,' Queen Elizabeth declared, with only a hint of sarcasm. 'Please sit beside me and let us converse a while.'

King James kissed her outstretched hand and sat down. Servants brought wine and dainty cakes.

'It is always a pleasure tae see yersel', Cousin Elizabeth. Ah am pleased tae hear you survived an attempt on yer life, and Ah'm glad tae hear oor mutual foe is nae more. Oor kingdoms are at peace, thanks be tae God,' said the king, as he raised a glass. 'These cakes are delicious.'

'Yes, Cousin, we are most thankful to God, and to your countrymen for their timely assistance. Sir Thomas assures me that things would have been difficult without them. He says the sight of a thousand highlanders screaming war cries, and the bagpipes a-playing, was enough to scare any foe,' she laughed. *Horrendous noisy things,* she thought to herself.

The king laughed. 'Aye, Ah have witnessed many such a charge. Sword and targe are fearsome in tha hands o' a Scot, for sure.

'Now, we must speak o' important matters, Cousin,' James continued.

'Yes, we must. I assume you refer to the succession. Should you outlive me, of course.' Elizabeth gave a glance at Sir Thomas. He smiled ruefully.

'Aye, the succession. Neither o' us is getting younger, Cousin Elizabeth. Tha matter must be made abundantly clear. If Ah survive you mah rightful succession is to be King o' England. James tha First o' England and Sixth o' Scotland.'

Sir Thomas interrupted, 'Yes, Your Majesty, but we do wish our beloved Queen many years yet, for sure.'

'But of course, Sir Thomas, Ah wish mah dear cousin long life, but death is a certainty, is it not?'

'Enough of this gloomy talk of dying,' the Queen declared, and she stood. 'Let us adjourn to the table and eat. I'm sure you are famished, Cousin. You do look a trifle peaky if I might say?'

James stood along with the others. 'Ah, ha'e been poorly o' late, Cousin, 'tis true. But Ah'm well enough now. It ha' been a few hours since Ah ate, sure enough. Ah hope Ah'll be likin' yer English food.'

'Venison is the same everywhere, Cousin,' replied the Queen sharply. She left without further comment and the rest all followed.

Fortunately, during the meal things became more amicable. Sir Thomas assured James that, should he outlive Her Majesty, parliament was totally in favour of his becoming King of England. *Better him than a Spanish one,* Sir Thomas thought. 'Parliament has even discussed a flag for the two kingdoms conjoined. I have taken the opportunity to request the Royal College of Heralds to submit designs for mutual approval.' King James nodded agreement.

Sir Thomas then proposed a toast, mischievously saying, 'A toast. To Her Royal Majesty – may she enjoy a long life and happiness.'

Everyone stood and repeated the words. King James did so with a scowl, quickly hidden, on his face. Queen Elizabeth smiled and gave a slight nod to Sir Thomas. No one at the table missed the implication of the toast.

***

A few days later James and his retinue returned to Scotland.

'Now, let us see to another important matter,' said the Queen. 'I refer to the traitor Stanley Dudley. I shall remove his title promptly…and his head in due course.' She chuckled, but no one doubted her intention.

'I have had his mansion searched and his servants questioned, Majesty,' said Sir Thomas. 'They said he departed suddenly when word arrived that the assassination attempt on yourself had failed. He was accompanied by a few others, presumably co-conspirators. The servants said they had been instructed to admit these persons without delay. There were five in total who spent hours in discussion.'

'Yes, these others shall forfeit their heads too. Do you know whence he went?' the Queen asked.

'To Ireland they thought but were not certain. It was all secret. Dudley, of course, did not say where they were going but he has contacts there among the local Irish nobles,' Sir Thomas replied.

'Hmm, you must leave at once, Thomas, and track him down. Take as many men as you think will be needed. A show of strength to deter any resistance,' the Queen said.

'I shall need about four hundred foot-soldiers. If needed I can get more when we land at Dublin, I hope.'

'Hmm, as you wish,' said the Queen.

The Queen continued, 'Now, it has been a long time since we enjoyed a play. Ladies, let us hasten ere we miss the first act.' She and her ladies-in-waiting bustled out of the room.

Would Master Shakespeare dare to start his play before the Queen arrived? I think not. Sir Thomas chuckled to himself. *Personally speaking, I find them rather tedious,* he thought.

Chapter 14
Have You Ever Been to Ireland?

It took some days to summon ships and provision them for an army. Four hundred foot-soldiers, and the horses for the officers, left the Thames in the spring of 1589 bound for Dublin.

'Have you ever been to Ireland, Sir John?' Sir Thomas enquired of Sir John Proudfoot as they stood on deck.

'No, never. I have heard many tales of the hazards there though,' Sir John replied. 'Bogland as far as you can see, it is said. Even wetter than England if that were possible.'

Sir Thomas chuckled.

''Tis a fair wind, Sir Thomas. We shall arrive in short time at our destination,' said the captain, George Alfredsson, of the ship carrying the leaders of the expedition. They were sailing westwards down the English Channel.

'Yes, I hope it stays calm, Captain. I was never a good seaman,' Sir Thomas replied. 'Give me a horse any day.'

'What I can do to make your journey comfortable is dependent on the weather,' replied the captain, smiling.

The weather changed abruptly as they turned north into the Irish Sea. Mountainous waves in St. George's Channel tossed the ships like corks. The horses were so tossed about that a few broke legs and had to be destroyed. Many of the men were totally discomfited.

The storm abated slightly the next day, but it was not until they entered Dublin Bay that there was a calm sea. A lot of soldiers were very thankful.

The ships docked and the slow procedure of unloading the remaining horses and supplies began. Sir Thomas's mare, "Beauty", had been one of the casualties. The men marched to the castle and settled in for the night. Those officers who had lost their mounts were soon supplied with replacements.

'One thing there is plenty of here in Ireland is horses,' quipped a stableman.

'Ah, Thomas, how good to see you again,' said Sir Henry Brocklehurst, the Governor of Dublin Castle. 'It has been many years.'

'Yes, too many, Henry. It is a pleasure to meet again, old friend,' Sir Thomas replied as they shook hands.

'I assume you are not here for a pleasure trip,' Sir Henry said, smiling.

'No, indeed not, Henry. We are in pursuit of a traitor, or rather, traitors. This letter from Queen Elizabeth will explain all, I think.' Sir Thomas handed over a letter in a sealed envelope.

'Her Majesty is well, I trust?' Sir Henry asked as he broke the seal and unfolded the letter. He sat down to read the contents. He thought a letter from the Queen deserved respect.

'Yes, Her Majesty is well and in good spirits,' Sir Thomas replied.

'Good, good,' said Sir Henry. He concentrated on the letter.

Whitehall Palace, London.
Ye six and twentieth day of March, Anno Domini 1589.

Dear Sir Henry,

We trust this letter finds you in good spirits.

I shall come straight to the point. I am sending my trusted friend, Sir Thomas Tovey, to Ireland on a matter of extreme seriousness. During the recent invasion of my realm, an assassin made an unsuccessful attempt on my life. The man was caught, I am pleased to say, and revealed, eventually, that he was in the pay of the former Stanley, Lord Dudley. I have been informed that this traitor has since fled to Dublin. Enquiries at seaports have confirmed this to be the case.

Sir Thomas must be enabled in every needful way to apprehend this traitor and any conspirators with him. I am certain you will not fail to assist.

Dudley is to be seized and returned to the Tower for execution. Should his death occur when being apprehended just send his head.

Signed this day,
Elizabeth R.

Sir Thomas sat and waited. Sir Henry thought for a while, saying nothing, then he called a servant for food and wine. 'Thomas, we need sustenance while we discuss this, this shocking news.'

***

After eating for some minutes, Sir Henry said, 'Stanley, Lord Dudley?! It is difficult to believe he is a traitor. Yes, he did pass through Dublin a few months ago. He was full of praise for Her Majesty and the army repelling the Spanish. I even supplied horses for him and his companions.' He shook his head.

'Companions?' asked Sir Thomas.

'Yes, there were five men with him. I don't recall their names. He said they were going as an embassy from the Queen to Ruairi MacLean, Earl of Glendalough, known as *Ruaidhrigh Ruadh*, or Red Ruairi, for his red hair. He has always been loyal to the crown, or so I thought.'

'Where is that, Henry?' Sir Thomas asked.

'Glendalough? Just beyond the Wicklow Hills, south of here. He has a small stronghold there I understand. A hundred or so men-at-arms, not more. He could of course have hired more. But he never gave any indication of being in league with any plotters. He has always appeared loyal to Her Majesty as I have said. I just cannot fathom why Dudley would visit him.' Sir Henry took another drink of wine.

'Well, Dudley and the five have gone there for a reason, no doubt. Of course, that is assuming they have actually gone to Glendalough,' said Sir Thomas.

'Hmm, yes, of course. There could be skulduggery afoot and there is only one way to find the truth, Thomas.' He raised an eyebrow.

'To go there,' Sir Thomas replied, nodding thoughtfully. 'I would admire it, Henry, if you could provide cavalry, maybe two hundred, and some cannon. Waggons for supplies as well. And I would be obliged for as many foot soldiers as you can spare. Are the locals behaving at present?'

'Yes, they have been quiet since the Spaniards were beaten, so your requirements will not be a problem. It'll give my men some battle experience. Garrisons grow fat and indolent doing nothing.' He laughed. 'Some small eight and four-pounder cannon. Anything larger will be nigh impossible to transport. Do you think the roads in England are bad? Wait till you encounter those hereabouts,' Sir Henry chuckled.

'Well, I shall take your advice, old friend. We shall leave on the morrow.'

'I will see that all is prepared.' Sir Henry then shouted, 'Captain Fitzallen.'

The captain entered. 'You called, Sir Henry?'

'Yes, Captain. Prepare two hundred horse, and as many men-at-arms and four and eight-pounder cannon as we can spare, plus provisions for them and Sir Thomas's men. Say, for a two-week campaign?'

'Yes, that should be adequate,' said Sir Thomas.

'Got all that, Captain?' Sir Henry said.

'Yes, Sir. I shall deal with it straight away,' Captain Fitzallen replied, and he saluted and left. He was a tall, well-built man of thirty years, with a commanding air. Much respected by the garrison.

'One of the finest officers I have ever had under my command,' commented Sir Henry.

***

Next morning the expedition set forth. Most of the garrison men were pleased to be doing something different to their usual guard duties, but a few moaned about leaving their warm barracks.

Half the foot soldiers were armed with swords and eighteen-foot-long pikes resting on their shoulders, the others wore swords and carried muskets, longbows or crossbows. They marched each side of the artillery and supply waggons. Two drummer-boys and a bugler were included to convey commands with drumrolls and bugle calls.

The April morning air was chilly but promised a warmer day. Trees were adorned with spring greenery and lambs frolicked in the fields near the city.

Sir Thomas, on his newly acquired mount, led the way. Some scouts were sent ahead to detect any ambushes.

'How good to be alive on such a morning,' he commented to his officers. They all agreed.

After some hours march, they halted for a meal of cold mutton at the edge of the hills.

'No sign of any enemy activity, Sir Thomas,' a scout reported. 'All is quiet so far.'

'Thank you, Soldier. We shall resume our way presently. Get some refreshment for you and your companions before you resume.'

'Yes Sir. Thank you, Sir.' The man knuckled his brow and moved to re-join his mates.

A half-hour later they resumed the march. Birds sang merrily all around them, until they were well into the Wicklow Hills. The hills were well forested, and trees almost bordered the narrow track they followed.

Sir Thomas commented, 'I can see why Henry preferred small artillery pieces. Anything larger would be a hindrance.' His officers agreed.

The scout Sir Thomas had spoken to earlier trotted back to the main force about two hours later. He was being deliberately casual so as not to alarm the column.

'Well, Soldier, what is the matter?' Sir Thomas enquired.

'Sir, a league ahead the forest is silent. Not a bird, not an animal to be seen. I suspect an ambuscade. I made an excuse my horse was poorly in order to slip back here. I have trained him to feign a limp. The others are awaiting my return. I am sure I saw men hidden stealthily in the trees, or a feeling in my gut, Sir, that all was not well.'

'You did well, my man. The foe will not attack them, or they would betray their plan to attack the rest of us,' said Sir Thomas. He turned to Sir John Proudfoot, his second in command. 'What think you, John?'

'Sir, I would advise great caution. The woods are not silent in spring for no reason. Might I suggest two parties, one on either side, to advance through the trees silently and attack the enemy from behind? Ambush the ambushers so to speak.'

'Yes, an excellent suggestion,' Sir Thomas said. 'Divide, say, a hundred men for each party to slip through the trees about five hundred yards from the track – the undergrowth is not too thick – that should mean they are well behind any ambushers. Impress on them the need for complete silence. All metal accoutrements to be removed, save their swords and shields or muskets. No pikes as they will be troublesome to manage in the trees.'

And so when all was ready the main party set off along the track. The two flanking groups being given a few minutes head start.

As they approached the spot the scout had left his men the main party adopted a light-hearted air as if nothing were suspected. Each man was, however, fully alert.

'What a fine day, Sir John,' Sir Thomas said loudly. 'Great to be alive!'

'Yes, indeed, Sir Thomas,' came the reply.

Suddenly, wild war cries rang out. A horde of Irish warriors charged from the trees on both sides of the track. The English army adopted their prepared strategy to oppose them; the pikemen lowered their pikes to deter the attack. They formed a row of vicious steel points along each side of the column. The clash of arms disrupted the peace of the forest. Many of the leading Irish attackers tried to pull back from the pikes but were thrust forward by their comrades and were skewered. Then the two concealed parties of soldiers fell on the Irish from behind. A volley of musket-fire surprised the attackers. The enemy realised their situation too late, and many fell to the sword but a few escaped and fled south.

'Shall we pursue them, Sir Thomas?' asked a captain.

'Nay, it will only exhaust our own men. Let the mounted men harry them for a few miles. That shall suffice. At least, now we know for sure Dudley and his friends are in the area.'

Chapter 15
The Stronghold of Red
Ruairi MacLean

The column proceeded across a marshy area where two rivers, the Avonmore and Avonbeg, literally Big River and Little River, meet in the Vale of Avoca. Spring rains had flooded the surrounding area; therefore it took some hours to get all the cannon to firmer ground.

Passing a round tower and monastic ruins near Glendalough the English troops came on their first sight of MacLean's castle, a modest stronghold. High walls surrounded the central keep.

It was situated on a mound overlooking the river Avoca and had several towers along its four walls. Two banners flew over it: MacLean's golden harp on a red background, and Dudley's white stallion, with golden hooves and mane on a blue banner.

'Seems we have come to the right place, gentlemen,' said Sir Thomas. 'Yonder flies the traitor's banner.'

'Aye, Sir Thomas, it is his all right. 'Tis a modest stronghold so we should overcome it easily. We should rest the men and commence our attack in the morning. Do you agree, Sir?' asked Sir John.

'Yes, indeed. Send a herald to the gate and ask that Dudley be surrendered. Declare that otherwise that castle will be destroyed. Not a stone shall lie upon another,' Sir Thomas stated.

'Very well,' Sir John replied. 'You, Captain Black, prepare a flag of truce and deliver that message.'

'Yes, Sir John,' replied Black, and he stuck a white cloth on a spear and rode to the castle gate.

'Ho, all ye within these walls, be it known that unless the traitors, Dudley and five others, be surrendered by daybreak, your castle will be destroyed and those within put to the sword. Surrender them and you shall live. What is your answer?' the Captain shouted.

MacLean himself, a short man with a thick red beard and hair, looked over the battlements and shouted down, 'Begone, you knave. I do not take kindly to threats. Do your worst.'

Captain Black sniffed contemptuously, turned his horse and trotted back to the English camp. 'He appears to have declined your terms, Sir Thomas.'

'I thought he might. Surround the castle. We start our attack at dawn.' He dismounted and went to his tent, hastily erected. 'Bring me food, for I have gained an appetite, this day.' He grinned.

***

Morning dawned and the besieged garrison witnessed the row of cannon which had been put in place overnight. The rising sun shone into their eyes forcing the defenders to shade them. The gunners stood ready to commence firing.

'A fine morning for a battle, eh, Sir Thomas?' declared Sir John.

'Yes, indeed, John. Is all prepared? Have the men been fed? Would not do to die on an empty stomach, what?' Sir Thomas replied in jovial mood.

'No, it would not. The men need to be thinking of the enemy, not their stomachs. All is in place. We only need your command to commence firing, Sir.' Sir John replied.

'Well, you have my permission. Give the signal if you would!'

Sir John, nodded to the bugler who began the "prepare to commence firing" call. Sir John raised his right arm and, when he had the attention of the gun commanders, he dropped it sharply. The guns immediately roared, and cannon balls battered the gate and walls of the castle. The wooden gate splintered in several places and masonry crumbled around it.

For two hours, the gate withstood the bombardment. The defenders had placed several large tree trunks behind it.

An Irish captain exclaimed to MacLean, 'Sir, we must attack the guns ere the gate is destroyed.'

'Hmm, very well, have a party leave by the sallyport on the south wall under cover of the smoke from the guns. Spike as many cannon as possible. The fools have not stationed infantry near their guns,' MacLean replied. He was more concerned than he appeared. He did not like the idea of his head adorning London Bridge. The heads of traitors were displayed there for all to see.

Stanley Dudley said, 'It appears your castle is not as strong as you led me to believe, MacLean.'

'Only a minor setback, Dudley, I assure you,' MacLean replied.

'Hmm, we shall see.' Dudley was hoping there was an escape route from the castle. Sir Thomas had sent soldiers to the other sides of the castle to prevent an escape.

Another salvo rang out from the cannon spreading a cloud of smoke towards the castle. The smoke lingered for some time as there was no breeze. Immediately some men ran from the sallyport to the nearest guns, killed the gunners and drove metal spikes into the firing holes.

'Stop them!' yelled Sir Thomas when he realised what was happening, but it was too late; many of the cannon were rendered useless. The enemy ran back to the castle.

'We should have been prepared for that,' Sir John added. 'That is going to extend this siege.'

Sir Thomas said, 'All the more shot and powder for the remaining guns. Increase the rate of fire – night and day if necessary. And get some of the musketeers and crossbowmen over there to protect the gunners.'

***

Gradually, the gate of the castle was rendered to virtual matchwood. The wall around it was badly damaged and the tree trunks only partly blocked the entrance.

'Now, we have them. Sound the charge!' Sir Thomas shouted. Another drum roll and a bugle call rang out and the infantrymen charged the remains of the gate.

'Won't be long now until the castle is ours,' shouted Sir Thomas.

'Yes, Sir, we are almost in,' replied Sir John shouting over the noise of battle.

The defenders hurled rocks and other missiles down from the battlements, but protective wicker mantlets, made from cut branches covered in cowhides, sheltered the attackers.

MacLean, Dudley and the other Englishmen retreated to the far side of the castle compound. Their men gathered around them.

'It is a fight to the finish now, lads,' shouted Dudley. The soldiers did not look too excited about the prospect. They looked at each other.

Ruairi MacLean shouted, 'We can still win, men, *Éirinn go brách!*'

The men replied half-heartedly, '*Éirinn go brách.*'

MacLean translated for the benefit of the Englishmen, 'That means "Ireland forever", Gentlemen.'

'Hmm, your men don't sound too forever if you ask me,' murmured Dudley.

He continued, 'MacLean, I'm sorry for getting you and your men into this. I had nowhere else to turn. Had we remained in England we would have been unjustly executed.'

'Think nothing of it, my friend,' MacLean replied. 'You aided me in the past when I needed this castle repaired. Your gold was very timely.' He smiled and they clasped forearms.

The roar of the besiegers interrupted their thoughts. The English troops, led by Sir Thomas, charged across the compound. The defenders readied themselves for the final battle, but some men looked at each other and one by one threw their swords to the ground.

'Pick up your weapons, you cowards!' shouted MacLean, but none listened.

One man shouted, 'Why should we die to protect these Englishmen?'

Soon all the men had laid down their arms. Dudley, his five comrades and MacLean were bewildered.

'You'll not take me alive,' MacLean shouted, and he charged the English soldiers shouting loudly. He was cut down by several blades and not a few arrows. His body lay oozing blood until he expired.

'Well, 'tis no matter. His head was not important,' Sir Thomas said. 'Bind those six traitors. The rest of you defenders, get out of my sight. There has been enough blood shed. You may thank God that I am feeling merciful this day.'

The defenders looked astounded. They had expected only death or at least maiming, usually loss of a hand. First one then the rest ran for the gate and headed into the forest.

Their camp-followers, womenfolk and families emerged from hiding and followed moments later.

Chapter 16
The Return to London

'So, whom do we have here? Stanley Dudley, the traitor, I know. Your names you swine?' demanded Sir Thomas.

The other five, heads bowed, gave their names in turn:

'Sir John Archer, from Suffolk.'

'Peter Cranley, gentleman, also from Suffolk.'

'Andrew Gainsford, gentleman, Kent.'

'Sir William Bedford, from Highbury, London.'

'Roger Davenport, gentleman, Cambridge.'

'Throw them in a waggon and let's be on our way. Burn this castle to the ground,' Sir Thomas ordered. 'Never again let it be used to defy the Queen's will.'

Some of his men lit bundles of sticks and fired all the buildings and the remains of the gate. The walls were demolished as much as time allowed.

Four hours later the party proceeded northwards to Dublin castle.

***

'Ah, Dublin's fair city at last,' exclaimed Sir John as they saw the buildings in the distance. 'A successful campaign, wouldn't you say, Sir Thomas?'

'Yes, very. I shall send a message to Her Majesty on the fastest ship leaving today. She will be pleased I'm sure. Maybe a monetary reward for you and me, Sir John?' said Sir Thomas.

'Or perhaps a manor or two? A would admire a few thousand acres in Wiltshire or even Sussex…with a view of the sea! Ah, bliss. And it would please my wife no end, the Lady of the Manor!'

'Sounds good when you put it that way, John. May I call you John? No point in all these titles since we are comrades in arms, eh?' Sir Thomas replied, smiling.

'Most assuredly, Thomas,' Sir John grinned. They shook hands and laughed.

'What's got into them officers?' a passing soldier, Oliver Templeton, asked his friend.

'Who knows…who cares? I hate officers, me,' the other, Ralph Baker, replied and they laughed.

'Drink later, mate?' asked the first man.

'Aye, why not. As long as you're paying.'

'We'll see,' his friend replied. *No chance of that, pigs might fly,* he thought and smiled to himself.

***

Three days later, the English party and the prisoners embarked for London. They had a period of ideal sailing weather and soon were sailing up the Thames, banners flying from every masthead.

Sir Thomas and Sir John headed straight for the palace. The Queen was residing at Greenwich, which was nearby, and they could see the Royal Standard flying from a tower.

'Ah, how good to see you again, Sir Thomas, and you too, Sir John,' said the Queen enthusiastically. 'You have met Master Shakespeare?' She indicated a tall person who had been sitting next to her. 'He has been outlining his latest play to me. Another about one of my ancestors!' Shakespeare stood and bowed but refrained from speaking. He had a sore throat.

'A pleasure to see you again too, Majesty,' Sir Thomas said and bowed deeply. 'And yes, I have had the pleasure of meeting Master Shakespeare before. Good morning, Will.'

'Good morning, Thomas,' Shakespeare croaked, and they shook hands. 'You have had a successful trip to Ireland, I hear.' He coughed.

'Yes, very successful indeed. Six traitors apprehended! All's well that ends well. Is that not so?' Sir Thomas replied.

'Hmm, I might use that as a title for a new play,' Shakespeare mused. 'Yes, "All's Well that Ends Well". I like it.'

'Wonderful news,' said the Queen. 'Do take a seat and recount your campaign, Sir Thomas. Bring wine,' she ordered a servant.

Sir Thomas then recounted the siege and taking of MacLean's stronghold. The Queen was enthralled.

Master Shakespeare wondered if that also could be material for a future play. A brave hero, and a good plot of treason and a retribution for the traitors, always went down well with audiences. He made mental notes.

'I am pleased to hear that only a few of our men were lost and that all the traitors have been apprehended. In the Tower now, I presume?' asked the Queen.

'Yes, Majesty. They go on trial in two days' time. The verdict is, shall we say, not in doubt. They have plotted against their rightful monarch citing your late father's divorce, it seems, and led a rebellion, albeit small, against your rule, Majesty,' replied Sir Thomas.

'Let us hope the verdict is as you predict, Sir Thomas,' the Queen replied, with a smile that implied trouble were it to be different.

***

'This court is now in session the Honourable Justice Goodheart Williams presiding,' intoned the Clerk of the Court sitting at Westminster Hall in the Palace of Westminster. The judge's parents had no idea how their son would fail to live up to his name!

A large venue was used for a great crowd was expected. 'Silence in court. God save the Queen.' The Clerk's words echoed around the stone walls and wood-beamed roof.

A hush descended on the crowd of jurors (twelve men) and public, anxious to see some executions.

The judge leaned down from his chair on a dais towards the prosecutor. 'Have the accused been put to torture?'

'Yes, My Lord, but all have refused to confess,' the prosecutor replied. He was surprised as most people confessed to anything to end the pain.

'Hmm, we shall have to proceed to trial.' The judge was hoping for a short session. 'Bring in the accused.' He sighed.

The six accused men, minus their titles, filed into the dock. Their lands and properties had already been confiscated by the Crown.

Each man had his left hand and arm wrapped in bandages oozing blood. A "glove" of leather and metal had been placed on the hand and screws tightened on each finger in turn. The flesh was pulped and then the bones broken one by one causing excruciating pain. The prosecutor was correct: few failed to "confess".

'I name the accused. Stand when your name is called,' said the Clerk. 'Stanley Dudley, John Archer, Peter Cranley, Andrew Gainsford, William Bedford, and Roger Davenport.' The six men stood with heads bowed. 'You are accused of inciting an attempt on the life of Our Sovereign Lady, Queen Elizabeth, of denying Her Majesty's right to reign by lawful succession, of aiding the army of an invader, to wit, the Spanish on their recent incursion, and of inciting a rebellion in Ireland. A rebellion, thankfully, put down by Sir Thomas Tovey. How plead you to these charges? Guilty, or not guilty?'

The six in turn said clearly, 'Not guilty.' There was much muttering among the people at this.

'Hang 'em!' a voice shouted.

'Silence!' The judge glared in that direction. He would not tolerate interruptions to proceedings.

'Is the prosecution counsel ready?' asked the judge, grim-faced and thinking this was a waste of time; an open and shut case.

'I am, My Lord,' replied Sir Archibald St. John. He was a thin, mean-faced individual. A smile had never been known to cross his face.

'Is the defence counsel ready?' asked the judge.

'I am, My Lord,' replied Percy, Viscount De Grange. A young man who was making a name for himself in the field of law. Unlike most viscounts, he lacked money, and so he worked for a living.

'Proceed,' said the judge.

Sir Archibald stood and said, 'My Lord, members of the jury, these six have conspired to remove our rightful monarch from the throne, for some as yet unknown reason. They paid an assassin to attempt to murder Her Majesty. They claim not to have desired a Spanish victory, which is a small consolation, but nevertheless it is still treason. Of that there can be no doubt. No justification at all. I demand therefore that you find all six guilty.'

The judge said, 'Will defence counsel make his statement?'

The Honourable Percy, Viscount De Grange stood. He addressed the court.

'Thank you, My Lord. Members of the jury, I have the pleasure of representing these six innocent men...' There were cries of protest from the spectators.

'Silence!' roared the judge. 'Another interruption and I shall clear the court.' The judge was sure of the guilt of the men but made sure that the defence could make their case.

De Grange said, 'As I was saying, these men have been viciously tortured as the jury can see, yet none has confessed. Not one, Gentlemen, not one.' The jury nodded.

'I shall demonstrate to you why it is extremely unlikely that these men are guilty of any crime whatever. They are, in fact, the victims of a dastardly plot. More of this later. I shall call witnesses to this fact, and I am certain, Gentlemen, that you will declare a not guilty verdict. Thank you, My Lord.' He resumed his seat.

The judge, looking sceptical, cleared his throat. 'Ahem, Sir Archibald, call your first witness.'

Standing slowly and strolling forward to the centre of the hall, Sir Archibald spoke loudly and clearly, 'I call Sir Thomas Tovey to the stand.' Sir Thomas stood and took the single seat in the centre of the trial area of the hall, facing the judge and jury. He was wearing a new dark blue jerkin trimmed in fur. His hair had been neatly brushed and arranged just so. He looked, in his own eyes at least, the picture of an honest man. He was sworn in.

'Sir Thomas, will you recount the events of the morning, the infamous morning, when an attempt was made on the life of our beloved monarch, and the circumstances which led to the arrest of the defendants?'

Sir Thomas cleared his throat, 'My Lord, gentlemen of the jury, while Her Majesty was residing at Warwick Castle during the recent invasion, an attempt was made on her life by a lone assassin. He used a knife,' – he indicated a servant to show the knife to the jury and the judge – 'which is no ordinary knife as you can see. It is an expensive weapon, of quality, which few could afford, especially an ordinary man.

I therefore concluded the assassin was backed by a wealth person or persons.

'Moreover, My Lord, an identical weapon was used to murder one of my employees, who had brought information on the Spanish army across the Channel.' Murmuring followed amongst the public. 'I therefore contend that the person or persons behind this plot are traitors in league with Spain!' There followed several minutes of uproar in the hall.

'Silence!' shouted the judge.

'The would-be assassin confessed and proffered a name before he, erm, died,' said Sir Thomas.

'And what name did he say?' asked the judge leaning forward in his chair.

'He named,' Sir Thomas paused for effect, 'Stanley, Lord Dudley!' All eyes focused on Dudley.

'What happened then?' asked Sir Archibald.

'In case, the assassination failed I learned that Dudley and his co-defendants were also plotting to overthrow the Queen by claiming the divorce of her father, King Henry VIII, was against the laws of the Church. This would have left only the late Queen Mary as the only legitimate monarch. After her death, the throne would have been claimed by her husband, Philip of Spain!' Horrified shouts throughout the hall. 'It was fairly common knowledge that the conspirators opposed the divorce. I shall go into this in more detail later if required.

'I then pursued Dudley and the other defendants to Ireland, whence they had fled, and apprehended them after a siege. A siege wherein several of Her Majesty's subjects perished. The six were returned under guard to London. That is all, My Lord.'

'I have no more questions, My Lord,' said Sir Archibald.

The judge said, 'Viscount De Grange, do you wish to ask the witness any questions?' asked the judge.

'I do, My Lord. Sir Thomas, who informed you of this imaginary divorce plot against the Queen?' He looked around the room as he said the word plot implying it was fanciful.

'Erm, it was common knowledge. Many clergy had heard it spoken of.'

'Yet very few seem to have been aware of this plot. I for one had never heard it spoken of. I wonder if any in this hall had heard of it?' He looked around but most people shook their heads. 'Hmm, common knowledge indeed!

'Turning to another matter; the identical knife you said was used in a previous murder. Where is this knife now?' Viscount De Grange asked in a sceptical tone.

'Erm, it has, erm, gone missing, Sir. One of the soldiers present may have taken it. I have no knowledge of its whereabouts,' Sir Thomas declared.

'Hmm, how very strange. My Lord,' De Grange said, looking at the judge. 'No more questions, My Lord.'

'Thank you. Sir Thomas, you may step down,' said the judge. Sir Thomas resumed his seat on the public benches. Lots of back-slapping from his friends.

'Have you another witness, Sir Archibald?' asked the judge.

'My Lord, I would call the Queen's ladies-in-waiting.' He then asked the three ladies in turn, who were present at the assassination attempt, to recount what had happened. They all told the same story of how the man was caught and subsequently died, after naming his paymaster.

'My Lord, I see no reason to call Her Majesty as a witness, so I shall call no other witnesses at the present time,' Sir Archibald sat down.

'Thank you, Sir Archibald,' said the judge. 'Viscount De Grange, have you any witnesses whom you wish to call?'

Percy, Viscount De Grange, stood and tried to look calm though his heart was racing. This was his first major trial. His first involving the nobility.

'Thank you, My Lord. I have but little experience of the law; I studied it at Cambridge, so please excuse my faltering and errors,' said De Grange. Sir Thomas and Sir Archibald glanced at each other and looked pleased.

The judge sat back steepling his hands and thought that this would not take long. *Proceed and make a fool of yourself, sirrah*, he thought. 'Proceed,' he said.

Viscount De Grange spoke and in a strong voice said, 'My Lord, and honourable gentlemen of the jury, these six are but loyal Englishmen and true to the Church here established by the late King Henry, of blesséd memory. I refer of course to the Church of England and that is why they were in no way supporting the Catholic Spanish king. Let us be clear about that.' He paused. There were murmurs and nods of approval around the vast hall. 'They were not, I repeat not, involved in any assassination plot, regardless of what Sir Thomas claims. This I shall prove, shortly.' He looked pointedly at Sir Thomas who began to have doubts as to what was to unfold. The judge sat forward eager to hear what the defence had in mind.

'I call my first witness just to clarify a matter. I call Sergeant Edward Jenner to the stand,' said De Grange.

'Jenner was present when Mistress Askew, the spy Sir Thomas referred to, was murdered.'

Jenner was sworn in and took the seat as a witness.

'Sergeant Jenner, how were you involved in the case of a killing of a young woman in London prior to the Spanish invasion?' De Grange asked.

'I was, Sir, in charge of the barracks when the young woman was rescued from a mob, her being mistaken for being Spanish. I had her locked in a cell for her own safety. The following morning she was found dead, a knife in her back. It had been thrown from a window in the cell. It was a very expensive looking weapon, Sir.'

'And what became of this weapon, Sergeant?' De Grange asked.

'That I don't know, Sir, for Sir Thomas took it away, he did.'

'Hmm, Sir Thomas took it away!' He looked at the jury to make sure this registered with them. 'But you would recognise the knife, should you see it again, Sergeant?'

'Oh, most certainly, Sir. Very ornate, very top quality it was, Sir. Owned by a rich man without a doubt.'

Viscount De Grange went over to where the weapon used to attempt to kill the Queen was placed.

'Could this be the weapon you saw, Sergeant?' He showed the knife to the sergeant.

'Aye, that is it. It certainly is the same one. Yes, I'm sure it is. There is a tiny nick on the blade, just there,' Jenner stated firmly as he pointed at the blade. De Grange walked over and showed the blade to the jury.

'And yet, Sir Thomas has said this is a different weapon, and he has no knowledge of the whereabouts of the previous one. As the witness has said, Sir Thomas took the previous knife away. It leads one to wonder if the two knives are one and the same, does it not, Gentlemen of the jury?'

'Objection, speculation, My Lord,' cried Sir Archibald.

The judge thought for a second. 'Overruled. It is a valid point, I think. I am most curious as to how this weapon is identical to the first weapon. Surely, such an expensive weapon would be kept safe!'

'Thank you, My Lord,' said De Grange.

The judge said, 'Sergeant, you may step down if the Prosecution have no questions?'

'No questions, My Lord,' said Sir Archibald.

'I thank you for your testimony, Sergeant,' said De Grange.

'It was no trouble, Sir,' and Jenner left the hall. He never liked Sir Thomas.

Viscount De Grange walked over and stood in front of Sir Thomas.

'Sir Thomas, you have heard what Sergeant Jenner has said. What say you to this? Where is the first weapon, or is this knife the only one, reused by the assassin, erm, would-be assassin?'

'I...I don't know. It...it was mislaid I suppose. That one is a different weapon. It is just a coincidence they are similar,' Sir Thomas blustered. The jury was sceptical.

'Hmm,' said Viscount De Grange. He looked at the jury to make sure they had appreciated the point.

'I call Lord, erm, the former Stanley, Lord Dudley to the stand,' De Grange said.

Dudley was sworn in. 'Master Dudley, I shall address you this way as your title has been removed even before this trial. *Homo praesumitur bonus donec probetur malus.* A man is innocent until proven guilty" the Law states.' De Grange paused. 'What was the nub of your discussions on divorce, royal or otherwise?'

Dudley, who was shaking and in considerable pain from his mutilated hand, nevertheless spoke clearly. 'The contention on the royal divorce was only an academic or theological exercise. That is all that it was intended to be. The Archbishop of Canterbury and the other bishops at the time, in the year 1533 if memory serves, permitted the remarriage of divorced persons while the former spouse still lived, to facilitate King Henry's divorce from Queen Catherine of Aragon, his first wife.

'The thinking was that as the king had married his late elder brother Prince Arthur's widow, it was not a true marriage. I think the biblical backing for this was a misreading of the text for expedient reasons; that a man could not marry his brother's wife. I am right, I think, in saying this was the idea put forward. Obviously, it would not be right for a man to marry his brother's wife while he was still alive!' Some chuckles from the spectators. 'However, Prince Arthur, Prince of Wales and Duke of Cornwall, was deceased and she, Catherine, was therefore a widow, so the biblical text obviously did not apply, in my humble opinion. Anyway, this was used as the reason for the divorce and King Henry was able to remarry...several times!' Some laughter from the crowd. The judge frowned. Dudley resumed, 'So, our question was – as indicated in the Book of Common Prayer when folk are married, that it be, "until death us do part" – is only the king's first wife, Queen Catherine of Aragon, to distinguish her from the other wives called Catherine, his true and only wife?

'Later wives, all five, were the result of the divorce obtained when he, the king, broke with Rome.' There were many nods of sympathy for this. The legitimacy of divorce and remarriage was contentious still. 'Can all subsequent offspring of those wives be true monarchs is the point of debate?' Dudley's voice rose louder as he spoke.

The judge interrupted, 'But, sirrah, that would exclude from the throne, Queen Elizabeth and the late King Edward, the Sixth of that name, true Protestant monarchs and Supreme Governors of the Church of England established by law, would it not?'

'Aye, unfortunately it excludes them both, according to this hypothesis,' replied Dudley. He emphasised the word "this". Many in the room were outraged. Edward VI was highly regarded by many. Dudley held up a hand for silence. 'It is unfortunate, but the question of the divorce affects all who succeeded King Henry, apart from his daughter Mary, born of Catherine – the first Queen Catherine.' Again there were some chuckles. 'This includes, by default, Queen Elizabeth who presently sits enthroned, and her half-brother Edward! Yes, but before you protest, Queen Mary had many faults, but she was the legitimate monarch, she being the daughter of his first marriage.'

'Order, order,' shouted the judge. There was uproar because Queen Mary was much hated. 'I shall not tolerate outbursts from the spectators. I shall clear the court if they reoccur. Continue, Master Dudley.'

'I predict, gentlemen, that in the near future the Church of England will exclude divorced persons from remarrying in a church, while their former spouse is still living. Queen Catherine's former spouse, Prince Arthur, was deceased as I have said. They had been married but six months when the prince was taken by illness.

'The divorce granted to King Henry, for the purposes of this discussion, makes all of his children ineligible as monarchs except Mary, his first born. I remind you, gentlemen of the jury, that this is just a theological concept and is not in any way directed at our present monarch. According to this hypothesis it is preferable to have a king or queen who has not been made so by divorce.' Cries of approval and disapproval came from some voices.

Dudley held up a large Bible given to him by De Grange. 'Moreover, in the Book of Malachi chapter two, and the fifteenth and sixteenth verses thereof it reads, "Let no one be faithless to the wife of his youth, for I hate divorce, says the Lord God of Israel". There we have it plain and simple, plain...and...simple, God hates divorce. But, as I have said, this is not intended as an attack on our gracious lady Queen Elizabeth, but only a subject for a Church debate.'

'But what of the allegation of attempted murder on her person?' asked Viscount De Grange.

'We had no part whatever in that, Sir. It is a fabrication dreamed up for reasons of greed, in my opinion,' said Dudley. He looked pointedly at Sir Thomas.

'Greed?' De Grange queried. He looked directly at the jury.

'Yes, Sir, my lands in Norfolk, which *adjoin* Sir Thomas Tovey's estate, have already been seized and earmarked for himself, should I be found guilty. I have no doubt the lands of my friends have also been so earmarked!' Uproar followed. Even the most ardent Tovey supporter could see the implications of this.

'This is a disgraceful accusation,' Sir Thomas jumped to his feet and shouted. 'I have had no part in any arrangement of land. I am as appalled as any of you. I am not a land-grabber.'

'Order, order,' shouted the judge. Gradually things calmed down. 'Sir Thomas, sit down.'

'No more questions at this time, My Lord,' said De Grange.

'Sir Archibald, do you wish to question this witness?' asked the judge.

'Yes, My Lord. Who then would be monarch, in your opinion, Master Dudley?' Sir Archibald St. John asked, trying to put Dudley on the spot.

'Under this thinking, and it is only a debate, the true king, by right of succession, is King James of Scotland!' The room was in turmoil at this. Most knew that King James would inherit the throne of England someday, but this was too much. Others were convinced that Dudley was right. Dudley resumed speaking. 'When Henry VIII died, his heir should have been his daughter Mary, not Edward. After her death in 1558, the throne should have passed to…' he paused, '…to the late, tragic Mary, Queen of Scots and then to her son, James VI. But this is only a hypothesis. I emphasise this, My Lord.'

Near pandemonium ensued. Some cried, 'Traitor!' but others cheered.

'James is the rightful king!' a voice cried from the back of the room. Others took up the chant.

The judge shouted for order. He was largely ignored, and the men-at-arms stepped forward and separated the two rival groups. A few heads were knocked about.

Sir Thomas sent a message to the Queen to inform her of proceedings. She was outraged.

'As the law stands,' said the judge when all was quiet, 'Elizabeth is our Queen and therefore an act against her person is treason. Any quibble about a divorce is of no account in the eyes of the law. Members of the jury, you shall ignore this assertion by the accused.'

Sir Archibald then said, 'My Lord, might I ask the defendant another question?'

'Yes, of course,' replied the judge.

'Master Dudley, why did you and the other five defendants flee to Ireland, if you are innocent as you claim?'

Dudley replied, 'A complete stranger arrived' – he looked directly at Sir Thomas to imply a link – 'at my home and handed me a message with a warning that I was accused of a plot, treason, along with my five friends.' He waved a sheet of paper in the air. 'This message states that we had been named by a person who had tried to kill Her Majesty. Rather than risk a trial and the execution required by law, I and my friends fled. One was very aware that evidence could be fabricated, or obtained under torture, My Lord.' Dudley looked at the judge and held up his mutilated hand.

'No more questions, My Lord,' said Sir Archibald.

'Have you any more witnesses to call, Viscount De Grange?' asked the judge.

'I call Master Norbert Donaldson to the stand,' Viscount De Grange said loudly.

Sir Thomas sat up with a start. *Why has he been called?* he wondered.

Donaldson was sworn in, and De Grange asked, 'Master Donaldson, in what capacity were you employed in Warwick Castle?'

Not knowing for certain what "capacity" meant, Donaldson said, 'I was a general handyman. I did lots of things, I did, Sir. Whatever the Earl or his good lady required.'

'On the occasion of the attempted assassination of the Queen, did Sir Thomas give you a special task?'

'Aye, that he did. I was to get a name from the murderer, attempted murderer that is. The name of him what paid him,' said Donaldson.

'What means did you use?' De Grange asked.

'I only had the irons from the forge, Sir. I am not used to that kind of thing. I heated them up in a fireplace to red-hot, I did, and held them to his body. Took a while but the swine was soon ready to talk. I did a good job on him, I did, if I might say?'

'And what did he say, Master Donaldson? Whom did he name?' De Grange asked.

'That I cannot say in all honesty, Sir.' Donaldson glanced at Sir Thomas.

'You cannot say!' De Grange exclaimed and looked around the room. Everyone was puzzled. 'Why not, Master Donaldson, may I ask?'

'Sir Thomas told me, and the soldiers, to take a break, to go for a drink 'cause the prisoner wished to speak to him alone. When we returned some minutes later, the man was dead. Dead as a doornail, he was.'

'So, only Sir Thomas heard the name of the alleged paymaster of the wretch?' De Grange asked, and he looked directly at Sir Thomas. Everyone looked at Sir Thomas.

'Aye, it were only him,' Donaldson replied. 'No one else was in the room.'

'No more questions, My Lord,' De Grange said.

The judge asked, 'Sir Archibald, do you wish to question the witness?'

Sir Archibald stood and said, 'Not at this time, My Lord.' He was aware that the facts were true.

'Thank you Master Donaldson, you may go,' Viscount De Grange said.

De Grange continued, 'Gentlemen of the jury, I would like to consider why Sir Thomas would then proceed to accuse my client of being the paymaster.'

'Objection, My Lord. Sir Thomas is not on trial,' said Sir Archibald.

'Overruled. This is interesting,' said the judge.

'Thank you, My Lord. This is relevant as my next witness shall prove. No one else, as you have heard, heard the confession of the miscreant. We have only Sir Thomas's word.' De Grange made a face of disbelief raising his eyebrows. 'Let me propose a reason. Master Dudley's extensive lands in Norfolk as we have heard, excellent farming land, adjoin that of Sir Thomas near King's Lynn. It is no secret that he has coveted that land for years, Gentlemen. My client refused to sell and now Sir Thomas has found a way to have those lands confiscated. I have been reliably informed that, should Master Dudley be convicted, he will be given said lands as a reward.' Viscount De Grange paused as the hall broke out in a hubbub. Sir Thomas's mouth opened and shut like a landed fish.

'Moreover, Gentlemen of the jury, I am given to believe that the lands of the other five defendants are partly to go to Sir Thomas.'

De Grange paused to take a sip of wine to let this fact sink into the jury's minds.

'Now, shall we come to a very interesting witness, Gentlemen? I call Mistress Daisy Lyttle to the stand.' Sir Thomas was wondering whom she might be.

Daisy Lyttle, a stick-thin young woman of nineteen years was wearing her best dress for the occasion. Apart from her work clothes it was her only dress. On her head was a white linen mop cap. She approached the chair timidly and sat down. She was trembling visibly as she was sworn in.

Viscount De Grange spoke kindly, 'Mistress Lyttle, may I call you Daisy?' Daisy nodded. 'Do not be scared by all these gentlemen, Daisy; they won't bite, not even the judge.' Daisy giggled and relaxed. They only wish to hear the truth. Tell the court what you saw and heard on the terrible day there was an attempt on the Queen's life.

'Will you tell the court where you are employed; where you work?'

'I be working in Warwick Castle, Sir. I be a scullery maid and general household maid, Sir.'

'So, Daisy, on that day where were you exactly?' De Grange asked.

'I was a-scrubbing the floor in t' gallery above the great hall, Sir. Someone had been sick and spilled wine and I was ordered to clean it. I had to wait till the Queen and her ladies went out into t' garden.'

'So, what happened then, Daisy?'

'Well, there I was down on me knees a-scrubbing the floor, when Sir Thomas and some soldiers burst into the hall dragging a man. I heard him being accused of trying to kill the Queen, Sir. I was shocked, I was,' Daisy said.

'And then what happened?'

'Sir Thomas ordered the man to be tortured to tell who had sent him. He called for Nobby, erm, Master Norbert Donaldson, to do the torturing. I was so afraid of being found in t' gallery that I just froze on the spot, Sir. I hardly dared to breathe. Then the man was stripped to the waist and tied down on a table. Master Donaldson heated some irons in t' fire and started to burn the man. He screamed something awful Sir. I felt sick. The smell of burning was something horrible...horrible.'

'Then what happened, Daisy?' asked Viscount De Grange, speaking kindly.

'Well, that went on for ages, must have been half an hour. Well, for a few minutes at least, then the man said he would talk but only to Sir Thomas. Sir Thomas ordered the other men and Norbert out of the room, then the man said something very odd...'

'What was that Daisy?' All ears were pricked up around the hall.

'He said, as near as I can recall: "You promised me gold if I did not tell your name, Sir Thomas. I have kept my part, now you must see I am released and give me my due". Then Sir Thomas replied: "Yes, you have, sirrah. I shall make it worth your pain and let you be released from this life", then he, Sir Thomas that is, put his hand over the man's face and pressed down. The man struggled for a few seconds then he went all floppy like. I realised he had died. I near fainted, Sir, I really did. I couldn't move. I was afraid I would be dead too if I were seen, Sir.'

'Then Sir Thomas called the others back in and said that the dead man had named a Lord Dudley as the one what paid for the killing, erm, attempted killing.'

'But the dead man had not actually said that name. Am I correct, Daisy?' De Grange asked.

'No, he never. He said Sir Thomas had promised him gold...' The spectators erupted with howls of rage.

'Hang Sir Thomas,' cried some.

'Chop his head off,' said others.

Sir Thomas rose to his feet and shouted, 'It's lies, all lies. You cannot take the word of a scullery maid against mine! I am a knight of the realm.'

The judge shouted for silence. Some guards prepared to restore order forcefully, but the men calmed down.

'Thank you, Daisy. You have been very brave. No more questions, My Lord,' said De Grange.

'Sir Archibald, do you wish to cross-examine the witness?' the judge asked.

'Erm, no, My Lord,' he replied. Sir Archibald was pale with shock.

Viscount De Grange said, 'Gentlemen of the jury, I contend that the would-be assassin named, or rather was speaking to his real paymaster, Sir Thomas, but was murdered before anyone else could hear. Sir Thomas Tovey seized the opportunity to accuse Lord Dudley and friends. I rest the case for the defence. Oh, just to add, I wonder why Sir Thomas accompanied the Scottish herald as far as Luton as he returned north?' He sat down.

Sir Thomas went pale.

'Thank you, Viscount De Grange,' said the judge, puzzled. 'Sir Archibald, do you wish to add anything?'

'No, My Lord. I have nothing to add.'

The judge said, 'Gentlemen of the jury, you have heard the evidence. Please adjourn to the room prepared and consider your verdict.' The jury filed out and sat in the room looking confused.

Chapter 17
The Jury Decides

Sir Leonard Grey, an elderly and distinguished man, a former Member of Parliament, who owned swathes of London, assumed the role of foreman of the jury. No one thought or felt inclined to oppose him.

'Right then, two things to be decided, Sirs. Number one: were the defendants plotting treason or was it only a theological discussion, or stance on remarriage as they claim? Two: as it is alleged Sir Thomas Tovey was the instigator of the attack may we assume the defendants are innocent?'

'Well then,' said John Ridley, 'it is an unexpected defence if ever there was one. The defendants seem to claim the divorce argument excuses their attempt to dethrone the Queen,' he said and looked around the others for agreement.

'Yes, and death is the judgement required,' added a juryman.

'The thing is, Sir Leonard, if one of us were to say anything in apparent agreement with what Dudley said, might one be accused of treason?' asked Jasper Frampton, a draper. He looked worried.

'A good point,' agreed Zechariah Milton.

Clearing his throat Sir Leonard said, 'Ahem, in the interest of justice shall we all agree that anything said in this room will not be held against that person, or repeated outside this room?'

They all nodded agreement.

'Very well. What is said shall only be regarded as a point of discussion, not allegiance to any cause.'

'Is there any validity to the assertion that the offspring of the late King Henry VIII, could have been excluded from the throne by the divorce?' Sir Leonard asked.

'Well, if the divorce meant that only the then Princess Mary could be monarch, then one could see that point as valid,' Frampton said.

'But does a divorce really mean that all later marriages and offspring thereof are invalid?' William Wells, a wealthy merchant asked.

'Hmm, surely not. That would mean no one who is divorced could ever remarry,' Sir Leonard said. Some of the jury nodded. 'If one can legally remarry, then the late King Edward, and Elizabeth, the Queen, are also rightful heirs of King Henry.'

Master John Ridley interrupted, 'The way I see it, none of this, divorce or no divorce, addresses the fact that an attempt was made to kill our Queen, God bless her. Surely that is what condemns the six defendants? Plus the possible link with Spain. Was it an attempt to crown James as King or Philip of Spain?'

A juryman said, 'The Queen's ladies-in-waiting all witnessed the attempt on Her Majesty's life. They all said the man confessed, and Sir Thomas named Dudley.'

'But they were only repeating what Sir Thomas told them. Is that evidence?' asked Zechariah Milton. 'Especially considering the maid's testimony.'

'I agree,' said four of the jury in unison.

'Can we just accept Sir Thomas's word for it?' another man asked.

'Can we take the word of a lowly servant over a knight?' asked another man.

'It is treason,' William Wells declared. 'Why they wanted her dead does not really matter in the end.'

Sir Leonard continued, 'Now, if there is any possibility Dudley and his followers are guilty of treason, the question remains, who else was involved: the Scots or the Spanish?' Some of the men were sceptical.

Jasper Frampton said, 'The Scots fought on our side and King James, as things stand, will be King of England sooner or later – much later one hopes.' Smiles of amusement at this. 'So, why would they be plotting? Why would they waste money hiring an assassin? And what did that lawyer mean when he said Sir Thomas travelled with the Scot?'

'Probably just a red herring,' said Sir Leonard.

William Wells commented, 'That only leaves the Spanish. Six men could hardly force a change of monarch on their own. They must have had a replacement king in mind.'

'And, presumably, that king was in on the plot,' Sir Leonard agreed.

'It must be the Spanish King. As Master Frampton said, the Scots have no reason to enter into a plot,' said William Wells. 'Her Majesty will die, like all people, at some time.'

'But Dudley said the divorce question was just a debate for the Church, not a plot,' Zechariah Milton asserted.

'He could just be saying that to cover his tracks,' John Ridley said.

'We just cannot be certain,' said Milton. 'There certainly has been a lot of talk about permitting remarriage for divorcees in churches, so perhaps it is true.'

'No, I have a feeling they planned to raise a rebellion against the Queen, and then to put James or the Spanish King on our throne,' insisted John Ridley.

'A rebellion? Really?' exclaimed Milton. 'Do you really think after the invasion and the Scots aiding us, that they could start a rebellion? Poppycock, total balderdash. The people are weary of war.'

'I agree,' said another juror. 'There is no appetite for more warfare, none at all. Why, some villages have no young men to till the fields, never mind fight battles!'

'Well, we cannot be certain beyond a reasonable doubt. So, assuming Dudley is telling the truth then Sir Thomas is blackening his name to obtain his land. It's possible,' Sir Leonard Grey said. 'People have done worse things for greed. We must tread carefully, or we could convict an innocent man, nay, six innocent men. And,' continued Sir Leonard, 'it would seem to me it was Sir Thomas who was behind the attempt. A strong possibility anyway.'

'Ahem, as was asked before, can we just take the word of a maid as against a knight?' asked Jasper Frampton.

'The lass was under oath, Sir. Seems to me her word is as good as anyone's,' said Milton.

Sir Leonard added, 'Yes, we cannot put a knight above the law. Why would the young woman lie? She has nothing to gain; and Sir Thomas has a motive; a lot of land to gain, it appears!'

'No one else heard the man's dying words. Sir Thomas had made sure they were alone, or so he thought,' added Milton. 'He is the guilty one, as far as I am concerned.'

'Yes, Sir Thomas is in line for being handed the confiscated land. He didn't deny it, did he? Moreover, why was the land taken before the trial? Innocent until proven guilty! Isn't that the maxim of the law? That's what the defence lawyer said.' added another juror.

'Let us vote on Dudley and company as regards the attempt on the life of the Queen; guilty, or not guilty?' asked Sir Leonard. 'Raise a hand for guilty.'

Four hands tentatively went up.

Ridley spoke, 'A point comes to mind: if Dudley is innocent, why did the six flee to Ireland?'

Frampton said, 'Dudley said a complete stranger handed him a message warning him that he was accused of a plot. Rather than risk a trial and execution, he and his friends fled. Why would a stranger do such a thing? Who could have sent him but Sir Thomas or one of the people in the Queen's entourage? This could indicate that Sir Thomas has deliberately implicated Dudley.'

'Hmm, it does sound suspicious,' added Milton. 'Who among us would stay around and risk trial for treason with the punishment thereof – hanging, drawing and quartering? Or a visit from Lady Axe? I think I would flee even were I innocent, especially with a rich and powerful man accusing me.'

'I agree,' said six other jurymen in unison.

'Let us take a vote to see where we stand,' suggested Sir Leonard.

Each man wrote "guilty" or "not guilty" on a slip of paper. The result was seven for not guilty, four for guilty and one undecided.

'Right, let us take a break,' said Sir Leonard. 'I shall ask the judge for guidance on this matter, for it all hinges on what was said, or not said, to Sir Thomas.'

***

'My Lord, may I seek your advice on the evidence given?' Sir Leonard asked the judge.

'Most certainly, Sir Leonard. What is the problem?'

'The jury wishes to know, whether it is advisable to accept Sir Thomas's word that the dying man named Dudley. There is no other evidence to support this. The maid said the man never named another person. Dare we condemn six men on the word of a man who has already claimed the property of a defendant? What one might call, a motive.'

'Hmm, you wish to question the word, under oath, of a knight of the realm?' the judge replied. 'Sir Thomas has always been an honourable man. Moreover he is the Queen's advisor, and the head of her security department. To doubt him could be construed as a slight on Her Majesty. Think on that, Sir Leonard.'

'Thank you, My Lord. I shall bring your words to the jury,' Sir Leonard bowed and left. *If we let Sir Thomas off, we condemn innocent men. If we condemn Sir Thomas, we could condemn ourselves,* he thought. *He is a man not to be crossed inadvisedly.*

***

'My friends, we are in a quandary, I'm afraid. Deep in a mire so to speak,' Sir Leonard said to the other jury members. 'The judge has indicated the difficulty of doubting the word of a knight, especially one who has the Queen's favour. We would place ourselves in a dangerous position.'

Milton spoke after a gloomy silence, 'But are we not duty bound to deliver a true verdict "beyond reasonable doubt" as the law demands? We dare not think only of our own welfare, Gentlemen. I could not live with my conscience if we condemn six innocent men to death.'

Again there was silence as the others pondered this. They all felt the burden of the situation in which they found themselves.

'I would like to hear from Sir Thomas about this liaison with the Scottish herald,' said another juryman, 'and the Spanish dagger. Had he kept the weapon?'

***

When the jury returned to the courtroom after their deliberations, they took their seats with worried faces. The whole hall waited, most people hoping for a series of executions.

'Silence!' ordered the judge. 'Has the jury come to a verdict on the case before them?'

Sir Leonard Grey stood feeling all eyes on him. He was never so nervous before in his life.

'We have, My Lord,' he said. 'But we, the jury, would like to have Sir Thomas questioned on the matter of the Scottish herald, and the Spanish dagger.'

The judge said, 'Perhaps later, Sir Loenard. Do you find the defendants guilty, or not guilty of inciting an attempt on the life of Queen Elizabeth?'

'Not guilty,' Sir Leonard said loudly. There was a stunned silence in the hall, then everyone started voicing approval or opposition.

'Silence!' the judge shouted. Gradually order was restored. Some guards threatened to draw their swords. 'Do you find the defendants guilty, or not guilty of plotting against Her Majesty, by questioning the late King's divorce, in order to incite a rebellion?'

'Not guilty!' said Sir Leonard. The crowd again erupted.

'The defendants are free to go,' said the judge. He was as shocked as the others at this turn of events, and said, 'Guards, place Sir Thomas Tovey under arrest. See he does not escape before I have time to question him.'

Sir Thomas tried to escape through a side door, but two guards grabbed him and hauled him in front of the judge.

'As it would seem you, Sir Thomas, have endeavoured to cover your crime by putting suspicion on six innocent men, for financial gain, I remand you in custody awaiting trial for treason. The nation is greatly indebted to the witness, Mistress Daisy Lyttle, for exposing this plot.'

Chapter 18
The Final Moments

One cold winter morning muffled drums were beating slowly, and guards lined Tower Green to keep the crowds of onlookers back, as Sir Thomas Tovey emerged from a building followed by a chaplain. He was reading aloud from the Psalms, 'Though I walk in the valley of the shadow of death I shall fear no evil.'

Sir Thomas, who had confessed to plotting with the Scots to enthrone King James immediately, stopped in front of the execution block, slipped a coin to the masked axeman to ensure a quick end, and spoke to the crowd. The Queen had mercifully decreed the axe rather than hanging, drawing and quartering, the usual punishment for treason.

The silence was eerie. 'I am come to the end of life having served my country to the best of my ability, but I have yielded to the approaches of the King of Scots to oust our sovereign Lady, Queen Elizabeth. He could not await the progress of time which would have made him King of England. I was tempted by Scottish gold. How true are the words, "The love of money is the root of all evil".

'For the sake of my immortal soul, I confess now, and regret most deeply, my endeavour to put blame upon Lord Dudley and his friends. I regret most deeply my attempt to betray Her Majesty and beg her forgiveness.'

At a nearby window in the Tower, the Queen wiped away a tear and turned away lest her ladies should see. *Alas that it should come to this, Thomas. My heart is heavy. My heart is broken,* she thought.

Sir Thomas continued, 'I now commit my soul to Christ's mercy and keeping. Farewell.'

He then knelt and placed his head on a wooden block.

The End

Ingram Content Group UK Ltd.
Milton Keynes UK
UKHW020625110523
421574UK00013B/419